Sweetheart Bride

Lenora Worth

Love Inspired

Recycling programs
for this product may
not exist in your area.

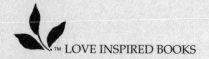

™ LOVE INSPIRED BOOKS

ISBN-13: 978-0-373-81672-9

SWEETHEART BRIDE

Copyright © 2013 by Lenora H. Nazworth

www.LoveInspiredBooks.com

Printed in U.S.A.

And the God of all grace, who called you to his eternal glory in Christ, after you have suffered a little while, will himself restore you and make you strong, firm and steadfast.
—*1 Peter 5*

To Linda White. Thanks for reading my books!

Chapter One

The soft sound of wedding music flowed through the quiet church. A hush fell over the crowd of people gathered to celebrate the wedding of Alma Blanchard and Julien LeBlanc. Candlelight gave the tiny sanctuary a muted, dreamy glow. The groom beamed a bright, loving smile as his bride seemed to glide up the aisle, escorted by her misty-eyed father.

Alma's older sister Callie, the maid of honor, looked radiant in a light golden silk dress with a flowing skirt. She smiled at her sister, her expression full of love and hope.

The other bridesmaid, wearing a similar dress with a fitted skirt, tried hard not to squirm and fidget. Brenna Blanchard sent up a little prayer for courage and self-control.

Dear Lord, please don't let me bolt out of this church.

She couldn't, wouldn't do that to Alma. Alma

and Julien were so in love. They'd been in love since high school, but circumstances and stubbornness had torn them apart for ten long years. It was their time to shine.

Brenna could hang on for a few minutes. As long as she didn't think about her own broken heart and the fact that technically, she should have been the one getting married, she'd be okay. Concentrating on the beautiful arrangement at the center of the aisle, she marveled at how her sister Callie could take sunflowers, mums and yellow roses and turn them into something exquisite. And what was the deal with all the Louisiana irises, anyway? Maybe Alma had a thing for irises?

Brenna forced herself into a serene pose as she smiled at her sister. Alma did look lovely in their mother's reworked wedding dress. Hadn't Callie worn that same dress on her wedding day? Wouldn't that sort of jinx the dress because she'd gotten a divorce?

No, this was their *maman*'s dress. Lacy and flowing and full-skirted, with a portrait collar. Beautiful.

Brenna's eyes misted over, the ache in her heart still an open wound. She wished their deceased mother, Lila, could see Alma now. She'd be so happy.

I'll be happy for you, Mama, Brenna thought now, her gaze scanning the crowded church. I won't be sad no matter how much I miss you, no matter how much I wish I could be the one walking up that aisle.

Brenna had a brief flash of pain, like a thorn from one of Callie's beautiful roses, as she thought of her ex-fiancé and wondered why she'd had love and lost it. Oh, wait, according to Jeffrey, her former fiancé, she wasn't good enough for him. He'd never said that out loud, but he'd shown it, loud and clear. Jeffrey *hadn't* said a lot of things, but she'd found out so much about him too late. Never again would she be interested in a man who held everything inside or kept things from her.

Never.

But in her heart she knew she really hadn't loved Jeffrey the way her mama and daddy had loved each other. She'd never loved him the way Alma loved Julien. She'd kind of stumbled upon Jeffrey and decided he'd make a perfect groom and a good husband.

Not. Maybe the brooding type wasn't her type, after all.

Brenna saw Alma's smile light up when her gaze settled on Julien, saw the way his grin went from happy to awestruck to humble with each step her beautiful sister took toward him.

I want that kind of love, she thought as she stood tall and held her head high. I want someone who will look at me the way Julien is looking at Alma right now.

Brenna glanced out into the crowd and locked eyes with a man sitting toward the back on the outside aisle, a man with dark hair and dark eyes, dressed in what else—a dark suit.

Who's the good-looking stranger? she wondered.

And why did he keep staring at her?

Who's the looker? Nicholas Santiago wondered, his gaze lingering on the second bridesmaid on the left. The bridesmaid who looked as if she'd rather be anywhere else but here.

She had hair the color of the tallow tree leaves falling outside, a rich golden-hued auburn that only burned brighter against the creamy gold of her dress. He couldn't see her eyes, but he'd guess they were a vivid green or maybe a vivid hazel. She shouted fire and heat, which probably meant she also liked a bit of drama.

Well, so did he.

But lately, he'd had too much drama. And coming to a sweet wedding simply because his new friend Callie Blanchard Moreau had invited him had seemed like a good idea when he rolled into town a few weeks ago. Now, Nick wasn't so sure. Too many bad memories.

"Please come, Nicholas," Callie had said. "Weddings are a good way to meet people. If you're going to be here for a while, you need to meet everyone. And we'll feed you. Alma insisted on cooking most of the food for her own wedding. You might even get a mention in Mr. Sonnier's 'Ain't that Good' column because he'll be here covering the wedding to help promote Alma's gumbo. You know, he's helping her to mass-produce it and sell it all over Louisiana. She hopes to expand in the next couple of years."

Callie was a talker, but the woman knew her flowers. And he'd need her help once he got the old Dubois estate, known around here as Fleur House, renovated for his picky client. They'd been good friends since he'd first come to Fleur a few months ago to check out the old antebellum mansion and purchase it for his secretive boss. Nicholas had remembered his mother's birthday, and Callie had helped him wire some flowers to her back in Texas. After they'd talked about the renovations at Fleur House and how he needed help decorating it, Callie had mentioned one of her sisters was an art expert. And that the sister would be at the wedding, of course.

So here he was, being courteous, being neighborly, by attending a quaint little wedding in a simple little church on a crisp fall Friday night.

And a good thing, too. He really wanted Callie to introduce him to that fidgety, adorable redhead and he sure hoped she was the sister who knew her art.

Brenna checked her lipstick and turned to head back in to the reception. The church fellowship hall was beautiful. Callie had outdone herself with the fall theme. And irises everywhere. She must have forced those to bloom this time of year, or found some that rebloomed in the fall. Callie could do anything with flowers. She'd managed to make this big, plain white room turn into what looked like a fall garden.

Shaking her head, Brenna rounded a corner and ran smack into *him*. The one she'd named Tall, Dark and Dark.

"Oh, I'm so sorry." He grabbed her by both arms, holding her steady while she stared up into those well…yes…dark eyes. "I should watch where I'm going."

"I'm okay," Brenna said, touching a hand to her upswept hairdo. "Nice reception, isn't it?"

How dumb could she be? Did he actually care about the reception?

He gave her a once-over. "Very nice."

Brenna hoped he didn't notice the blush popping out over her freckles. She did not blush prettily.

"See you later maybe?" He waved a hand in the

air and Brenna immediately noticed his expensive gold watch. So like Jeffrey's.

That turned her off enough to start walking away. "I should get back."

"Hey, don't leave in such a hurry."

He had a bit of an accent. Hispanic maybe. That would explain the hunky dark good looks.

She turned, smiled at him. What would it hurt to flirt with a nice-looking man? He wasn't wearing a wedding ring and…neither was she. She needed to stay in practice, didn't she? But she couldn't find the courage to have her heart stomped again.

"I have bridesmaid duties." She thought hard, but couldn't remember exactly what those duties might be.

"Very important job," he said, coming to stand with her while they gazed out on the crowded room. "The first being, of course, to stand around and look gorgeous?"

Brenna giggled. "You're not serious, right? I mean that's a line, isn't it?"

He grinned and the brilliance of it sizzled the paint on the walls. "Did it work?"

Well, she was laughing. That was something new. But Brenna didn't want to laugh. So no flirting, no laughing. And nothing left to say. Awkward.

"Oh, good, you two have finally met each other." Callie twirled and pranced toward them.

"Brenna, this is my friend Nicholas Santiago." She smiled at him, then touched a hand on Brenna's arm. "And this is my baby sister. I think I mentioned her to you. She's home for a while from Baton Rouge."

The man gave Brenna another one of those smoldering looks. "So you're the little sister. Wow."

"That's me," Brenna said, smelling a setup. "Wow. Nice to meet you, Nicholas."

"Nick," he said, taking Brenna's hand. "I was about to introduce myself. Once we got out on the dance floor."

Brenna bristled. "I didn't say I'd dance with you."

"But you will," her bossy sister said, pushing her toward Nicholas. "Don't be rude to my friend."

I...uh..."

But it was too late. They were suddenly moving across the dance floor to the tune of a Cajun-inspired waltz. Brenna glanced around and saw her sisters smiling and waving. She'd deal with them later. Her daddy, Ramon, waved to her from where he sat with Julien's friend Tebow and Tebow's mother. He'd been hanging out with that woman way too much lately.

"You have such an interesting family," Nicholas said. He wasn't looking at her family, though. He was looking down at her.

"Yes, they're very colorful and ever so helpful."

"You have a cute Southern accent."

Still looking at her.

So she stared back. "You have a different kind of accent."

"I was born in Mexico but moved to Texas when I was a teenager."

He said it with a thickening of his accent. *Me-he-co.* She almost missed a step.

"How did you wind up here?"

He laughed at her deliberate smile. "Good question." Then he whirled her around again. The man smelled like a fresh rain out on the sea. So good. No, not good. Not good at all.

Brenna pulled in her flaring nostrils. "Well, *what* are you doing here?"

"I'm an architect. I'm here to oversee the renovations on the Dubois house. We've been working on it for a month or so now. Just about finished with the inside."

"Fleur House." That got Brenna's attention. "Oh, I love that house. I used to go past there and wonder what kind of art was inside those old walls. I'd decorate it inside my head. I always heard Mr. and Mrs. Dubois had quite a collection at one time. Of course, I never actually got to go inside the house."

He gave her what looked like a teasing glance.

"Callie tells me you have a deep appreciation for art."

"Appreciate. Yes, more like a passion. I make my living from selling it," she replied. "I work in a gallery in Baton Rouge." Or at least, she had. "Budget cuts have forced me on an indefinite lay-off, however."

He nodded, inclined his head toward her. "Brenna mentioned that to me. It's good to know. I might need some help with the renovations. My employer will expect some world-class pieces and I could use a hand picking them out. I know what I like, but he has very refined taste and a big wallet to back it. And although he told me to surprise him, I need an expert." He winked. "I think you'd be perfect."

Brenna scanned the room for Callie. So she could murder her. "What a coincidence. Because I know my nosy sister wouldn't dare put you up to dancing with me just so we could discuss art, now would she?"

He actually looked confused and then he grinned. "No. I wanted to dance with you *before* I knew you were Callie's sister." Leaning close, he said, "I have to admit, I was hoping you were the art expert, however. I saw you fidgeting up there by the bride. You obviously don't enjoy weddings."

Brenna wanted to explain exactly why she

didn't enjoy weddings, but that would be rude. "I'm very happy for my sister, but weddings give me the hives."

"Oh, I see. You're not ready to settle down."

"I'm just not ready to settle," she said on a snap.

"Hmm, someone is bitter."

"Very."

"I'm sorry." He whirled her around the floor, bringing admiring stares from the onlookers. "If it makes you feel any better, I've been burned a few times myself."

"It should, but it doesn't." She didn't want to be mean, but this man was annoying. But easy on the eyes while he was being annoying. His suit looked expensive. His hair glistened like wet ink. And those eyes—part pirate and part heartbreaker.

Brenna was pretty sure she heard sirens and warning bells going off inside her head.

"I won't tease you anymore," he said, turning serious.

She changed the subject. "And as far as getting my advice on art?"

"I'm a businessman, Brenna. I need an art expert. Your sister was thrilled to tell me about you and how talented you are, but if you're not interested—"

"I am," Brenna said, wishing she could climb into the wedding cake and never come out. "I mean, I'm always interested in acquiring good art. But my expert opinions don't come cheap."

"I'm willing to pay you a fair salary," he said, giving her one last glance. "I enjoyed our dance. But if you'll excuse me, I have to get back to work."

"On a Friday night?" Brenna said, more to herself than him. She had actually begun to enjoy talking to him.

"Every night," he replied. With a wave and what seemed like a dismissal, he turned and left.

And Brenna realized the music had stopped.

Chapter Two

"Order up!"

Brenna skidded on her sneakers, then stopped an inch from Winnie. "Did y'all get that order for the Western omelet, heavy on the sausage and salsa?"

"Got it," the cook called through the pass-through. "Told you that five minutes ago."

"And my customer's been waiting ten minutes."

Brenna pushed at strands of damp hair. Filling in for her sister had seemed like a good idea a week before the wedding, but now her feet hurt, her back hurt and she needed a long hot shower. And it was only eight-fifteen on Monday morning.

How did Alma do this day in and day out?

"Got a new customer in your section," Winnie said with a smile. "You'll get the hang of it. It's like riding a bike."

"Yes, but bike riding is much more fun than

this," Brenna replied with an impish sticking-out of her tongue.

Then she glanced down the aisle and saw a gleaming dark head and a crisp white button-up shirt. "No, not him."

"What is it?" Winnie stared toward the table by the window. "Just a handsome man needing food."

Brenna lowered her voice. "Not just any man. Nicholas Santiago. I met him at the wedding. He made me...nervous."

"Oh, I see. I do believe you not only met him, but didn't you dance with him, too?"

"Uh...sorta. Only because Callie made me."

"Yeah, right." Winnie handed her a menu. "Well, we're busy, so you need to let go of being nervous and go make nice."

"You are no help," Brenna replied. "Look at me."

"I see you," Winnie said on a chuckle. "But I don't see those overpriced walking shoes walking toward that waiting customer."

"You're mean, too," Brenna said, but she couldn't hide her smile. Winnie wouldn't hurt a fly. Or at least Brenna thought she wouldn't. But Winnie would defend to the death anyone she loved. And Brenna knew Winnie loved her.

So she had to do her job and do it with a smile.

And pray he wouldn't recognize her.

"What'll it be," she said, staying off to the side. Hoping he wouldn't glance up.

He did. Then he grinned, the effort splitting that interesting face while she was pretty sure the sun split through the clouds outside.

"Hello. Bridesmaid number two, right?"

"Always the bridesmaid," she quipped, then instantly regretted it.

"And a woman of many talents."

She shook her head. "This isn't one of them. I'm helping out so my sister can enjoy her honeymoon."

"I see." He took his time glancing over her Fleur Bakery T-shirt and jeans. "Cute. Especially the 'slap-your-mama' part."

"Cute?" Brenna wanted to die. "I'm hot and tired and so not a morning person. I really do want to slap someone. But not because of good cooking, even though we do offer that." She hissed a sigh. "What do you want for breakfast?"

"Hmm." He kept his eyes on her. "How about one egg, scrambled, dry toast and fruit."

"You call that breakfast?"

He laughed, his eyes twinkling. "What would you suggest, then?"

"Eggs, country cured ham, biscuits that will make you weep for butter and some of Alma's mayhaw jelly with a big cup of our famous strong coffee."

"I'll take it."

She gave him a long stare, then grinned. "I

thought so." Putting her pen over her ear, she shot him a mock-sweet smile. "I'll be right back."

Nick enjoyed watching her work the room. She seemed to know enough to make a passable waitress, but he could tell this definitely wasn't her thing. He imagined her in a conservative suit with sensible but attractive high heels, her briefcase and designer purse on her arm. He imagined her dancing with him again and wondered why he couldn't forget the scent of her floral perfume.

Dangerous territory, this. He'd come here to do a job. And it was a big job. Probably one of the biggest renovations of his career. His client paid top dollar for discretion and design.

Nick intended to provide both.

But he did need someone to help with the art and decor.

Could he help it if the only woman in town he was actually attracted to also happened to be an art expert who was out of a job and waiting tables?

Coincidence? Or divine intervention?

His mother had been praying for him to settle down with a pretty woman so she could have grandchildren.

But wait, he'd come close only once or twice to having that perfect domestic life his family expected. Hadn't worked out so great. Maybe he should just focus on business. And try to forget the past, as his mother and aunt suggested every time he went home.

Brenna brought his breakfast and yes, the biscuits did look good. But so did the bearer of the biscuits. Although she looked completely different today from the way she'd looked at the wedding a few days ago, Brenna Blanchard was still a pretty woman. Her hair, caught in a big clamp, was falling in damp wisps around her face. He couldn't decide if she wore makeup or not, but that didn't matter. Her skin shimmered with a glowing sheen that made her appear young and carefree.

He quite preferred this look, actually.

Okay, strike that.

He liked her both ways.

Still dangerous. So he told himself to stop obsessing about Brenna and get on with his meal. The food was great, the service wonderful. He'd eaten here several times and he was sure he'd be back a lot before he was done with this job.

And he'd have plenty of opportunities to get to know Brenna Blanchard. He'd just need to remember it was all about the art for the house, all about pleasing his wealthy boss.

And not at all about remembering Brenna's silky hair and shimmering skin.

Brenna checked on her tables one last time. Saving Nicholas Santiago for last, of course.

"How was your breakfast?" she asked, noting he sat reading over some papers.

"Very good." His smile told the tale.

"Most people leave here with a smile," she said, glad she hadn't spilled anything in the man's lap. "Want some more coffee?"

"Only if you sit and have a cup with me?"

"I'm working here," she said, exaggerating the term.

"Don't you get breaks? I'd like to discuss what we talked about at the wedding. I really do need some advice on how to decorate this house."

She glanced around. "We're not too busy. Let me get a cup and I'll talk to you for a few minutes."

She hurried to the back of the counter and found Winnie. "Can I take a short break? I need to talk to Nick. He might have a job for me."

"Oh, it's Nick now?" Winnie giggled. "What? Tired of this cushy job already?"

"Never," Brenna said with a mock-smile. "But I need cold, hard cash. And he needs an art expert."

"A match made in heaven," Winnie replied. "Go. Who wouldn't want to take a break with that hunk?"

Brenna swallowed her trepidations and told herself she could be professional and businesslike. She would not mix any pleasure with this business. She needed work to keep her mind off her many failures.

"Okay," she said as she slid into the seat and poured herself some coffee from the pot she'd left on the table. "Fifteen minutes."

"I can handle that," he said. "Let's pretend this is a real job interview. Tell me about yourself."

Okay, now she was nervous. Sitting here in a T-shirt and jeans didn't feel professional. And she didn't have her résumé in front of her. "Well, I went to LSU in Baton Rouge, majored in Art History and minored in Business. For the past three years, I've worked in the Hutton Gallery as a curator and director of operations. But budget cuts caused me to be laid off indefinitely." She sat back against the booth. "As you've probably noticed, there isn't much in the way of art here in Fleur."

He nodded. "You don't appreciate the Fleur Bayou Museum?"

"Of course." She grinned. "I helped create that museum when I was still in high school. But I never could find anyone willing to keep it open on a daily basis. It's only open when Mrs. LaBorde's gout isn't acting up—which is a whole lot these days. So the museum is more neglected than noticed."

He burst out laughing, his dark eyes sparkling. "I think I met Mrs. LaBorde at the wedding. Charming woman."

"You're just being polite," she said, touched that he'd enjoyed her joke. "She loves working at the museum, but she does have a life, after all."

"And it is a small place," he added. "I checked it out the first day I arrived. I wanted to get a sense of the place. And now that I know you had a hand in the content of that one-room history trove, I'm doubly impressed."

"So did it help you to understand the history of this area?"

"It did."

He started asking her questions about the Cajun and Creole history of Fleur and the Spanish influence of the area. Before Brenna knew it, thirty minutes had passed.

"Oh, I have to get back to work! Sorry we didn't get to discuss Fleur House and what you might need from me."

He stood when she did, then reached out for her hand. "You're hired."

Surprised, Brenna took his hand and shook it. Or rather let him shake her hand. "But you don't even know if I'm right for this job."

"Oh, you're perfect."

Relieved and pleased but a bit wary, Brenna pulled her hand away. "And how do you know that?"

He gave her one of those simmering looks

again. "By the way your eyes lit up when you were talking about that little shanty museum you created. You love this area and you love art. That's all I need to know."

Her heart did a little flip of gratefulness. Jeffrey had never understood her deep love of history and art. He'd teased her about finding a real job with a real salary. He'd never appreciated the town of Fleur, either. Called it a hick-boonie town.

"So what do you say? Do you want the job?"

"Well, yes." Her heart raced with excitement. "That was easy."

"I think so, too. Because you're the first art expert I've interviewed today and probably the last, I'd say breakfast was a success."

"Thank you," she said to Nick. "When do you want me to start?"

"Immediately," he replied. "But you can wait until your sister is back. I know you're needed here."

"Good. I appreciate that. But I can put in a few hours at the house between the lunch and dinner shifts. Besides, Alma will be back next Monday."

"That should work out great." He dropped a twenty on the table. "I enjoyed the meal and the conversation."

Brenna didn't know what to say. "I'm glad you

did. I guess I'll see you Monday. Where should I meet you?"

"At the house," he said. "We'll do a walk-through." Then he touched her arm. "But aren't you forgetting something?"

"I can't think of anything," she said, alarmed. "Have I messed up already?"

He laughed. "Relax. You've done everything right. Except ask about the salary? Don't you want to know about the pay?"

Brenna breathed a sigh of relief. "I'd probably do it for free, but pretend you didn't hear me say that."

"I didn't." He smiled and named an amount. "Does that sound fair?"

Brenna tried to hide her surprise. He'd just offered her more than she'd made in a year for what should be a short amount of work. "More than fair," she replied. "And Nick, thank you."

"It will be my pleasure," he said, his gaze dropping to her face. Then he handed her a card. "Here's my number. I'll be in touch."

Brenna hurriedly scribbled her cell number on the back of a napkin. "And mine, in case you change your mind."

"I won't," he said. He gave her another devastating smile and strolled out of the café.

When Brenna heard a whoop and some giggles coming from the back of the restaurant, she hurried to do some damage control. Rumors would be flying, no doubt about that. She was in way over her head with this man. No doubt about that, either.

Chapter Three

Callie came waltzing into the café and strolled around the counter to pour herself a cup of coffee. "I hear Nick came by to see you this morning," she called to Brenna.

Cringing for the second time that day, Brenna shut the door to the supply closet and grabbed her smirking sister by the arm. "Do you have to announce that so loud they heard it in New Orleans?"

"Well, did he or didn't he come by?" Callie asked, her loosely knotted bun bouncing against her head. Why did she always have to be so perky?

"Yes, he came to eat breakfast," Brenna replied. "And how do you know this already?"

"I have my sources," Callie said, spinning on her short suede boots. She slid onto a barstool and did a matching twirl. "I knew you two would hit it off right away."

"We didn't hit it off," Brenna replied while she

stacked napkins into the nearby holder. "But he did offer me a good job."

Callie actually clapped. "Sounds like you did more than just *hit* it off. This is better than I expected."

Brenna held up her hand. "Whoa! Don't get the wrong idea. We clicked enough that I think I can enjoy working for him. The man offered me a huge amount of money, so yes, we got to know each other rather quickly."

Callie beamed with pride. "I told you he'd hire you on the spot, didn't I?"

"You did and he did," Brenna confessed. "It seems a bit too easy to me. I'm afraid there's a catch."

"What catch? No catch other than you'll be doing the work you love with a handsome man who also appreciates art and beautiful homes." Callie grabbed a piece of sweet potato pie and began to dig in with relish. "Oh, this is so good. I love Winnie's sweet potato pie."

Brenna giggled. "I can tell." She took a fork and had a bite, then dropped the fork onto a napkin. "I miss Alma."

"Me, too. She'll want to hear all about this. You and Nick, I mean."

"Hey, there is no 'me and Nick,' got it?"

"Got it," Callie said between chews. "I wonder

if he'll want children. Does he know you're kind of gun-shy in that area?"

Brenna slapped her sister on the arm. "Will you stop talking like that, please? I don't intend to marry the man. I just want a good job for a good day's work."

"And I just want nieces and nephews and another wedding to plan. And I wouldn't mind living at Fleur House, while we're wishing."

Brenna pretended to not notice the sadness in her sister's eyes. Callie deserved to be happy and she'd make such a wonderful mother. She said a prayer for her sister, then teased, "Get your own man. Preferably, the one who actually owns the house. I hear he's filthy rich and quite mysterious. He'll have to show up to claim his property sooner or later. You'd better be ready."

Callie shook her head. "No, I had my turn. One divorce is quite enough for me, thank you." She gave a dainty shrug. "But this mysterious owner is intriguing."

"So you'll just mess in my life to occupy yourself until the owner shows up?"

"Yep. Seems to be working. Wait until I tell Elvis. He'll be thrilled, too. He loves Nick."

Brenna finished filling napkin holders. "That big mutt loves anybody who breathes. But I can agree with your dog on one thing. Nick is nice-looking."

"Of course he is. Would I set you up with just any ol' body?"

"We are not set up, remember? We're working together."

"Got it." Callie finished her coffee and pie, then waved her hand in the air. "Just working together. Right."

Brenna shook her head, then finished her busy-work, her mind in turmoil at the thought of working so closely with Nicholas Santiago. She didn't even know the man and already, he was messing with her head. Telling herself to stick to the plan—business, business, business—she decided it wouldn't hurt to research her new boss just so she'd be familiar with his style and the demands of her job. She'd do that first thing when she got home tonight.

He'd research her, see what kind of credentials she had. Nick rarely hired anyone without doing a thorough vetting, but he had no doubt Brenna Blanchard would be an asset to his renovation team. She knew the area, knew the history and she seemed to have a passion for art and litera-ture—two things his boss demanded in all of his employees.

Nick remembered the pride she'd displayed when discussing Fleur and the surrounding areas. Brenna might not want to spend the rest of her life in her quaint little hometown, but she sure did care about the place. That was the kind of intimate passion he needed to renovate and decorate Fleur House. While he had a great interior designer ready to re-create and decorate the house, he also wanted a curator to oversee hanging the art pieces his employer already owned and to buy other pieces to complement the entire house and collection.

Brenna would do the job and he'd enjoy the fringe benefits of her delightful company. A win-win situation. Or one he'd regret when it came time to pull up stakes and leave. Which he'd have to do sooner or later.

Nick got up and looked out the window of his temporary home—a construction trailer parked behind Fleur House. The nondescript trailer served as an office and a place to stay. He'd designed it that way so he didn't have to rent out a room or stay in run-down hotels. And while Fleur had some quaint little cabins along the bayou, he much preferred to be alone in his own traveling home. He liked the privacy and the ease of transporting himself.

A quick, clean getaway.

That was how the last woman he'd left had described his mode of operation. Or rather, she had called his trailer a means of a quick and easy escape.

And she'd been so right.

He liked to get in, do the job and get out.

No ties to bind him. No hassles to hold him.

So why was he sitting here now doing an online search for any information he could find on Brenna Blanchard?

Because he needed to know her so he could work with her. Of course.

When he pulled up a society picture from the Baton Rouge *Advocate* newspaper, Nick pored over the words with a hungry intent. Dated a few months ago, the caption stated that Brenna Blanchard and her fiancé, Jeffrey Patterson, had attended a dinner to raise funds for a Baton Rouge art event. The note went on to talk about Brenna's position at the art gallery and Mr. Patterson's work at a Baton Rouge law firm. Nick quit reading after that, but he couldn't take his eyes off the woman in the picture.

Brenna, dressed in a shimmering dark blue cocktail dress, smiled up at the man next to her, her gaze bright with love and admiration. And happiness.

Fiancé?

Had she been engaged to this man?

If so, they must have broken up. Maybe that was why she was unemployed and back in Fleur. Her attitude regarding marriage indicated she wasn't the marrying kind.

And she wasn't wearing an engagement ring now.

So much for vetting.

Nick had more than enough information on Brenna Blanchard. She wouldn't stick around too long, either.

So he had nothing to worry about really.

She worried with the collar of her blouse.

Not sure how to dress for her first official meeting with Nicholas, Brenna waffled between jeans and a T-shirt to a blue button-up cotton shirt and dress pants.

She finally settled on putting the button-up shirt over some nice trouser jeans. Sensible cushioned loafers would be better than heels while walking throughout the house. She didn't want to listen to the tap-tap of her shoes while she was trying to envision art on the walls.

Or maybe she didn't want to distract her new boss with a pair of high heels because she planned on keeping this relationship strictly professional. But she did mist herself with perfume, just for good measure.

After researching him online, she'd found him only in a few professional pages, but his work reviews were all five-star. Clients raved about his work ethics and his professionalism. Apparently, he was that good. His client list read like a who's-who of prominent Texas tycoons. Only she couldn't find any reference to Fleur House or his current client. That was interesting.

She'd found something else interesting, too.

Nicholas Santiago was also an artist. Some paintings had shown up under the name Nick Santiago, paintings he'd done as a teenager. Or at least she figured it had to be the same Nick—her Nick? Well, not her Nick, but the man she'd agreed to work with. One of the paintings was of a beautiful dark-haired girl on a horse. She looked young and carefree. He'd won an award for it in high school.

"Jessica." That had been the name of the painting. Of course, now she wondered who Jessica was and what did she mean to Nick.

She'd seen another article, but Callie had called her and they'd chatted too long for her to go back and read that one. It had something to do with that painting, though. She'd have to remember to read that later. Right now, she had to get to Fleur House.

A few minutes later, she was in her car about to leave when her daddy, Ramon, came strolling out of the house. She loved being back here with her father. She tried to pamper him as much as she could, but her overly protective father seemed to think she was fifteen again. So he lectured her. And worried about her.

Brenna cranked the car and tried to make a quick exit.

In spite of his bad knees, he shot down the brick steps of the white clapboard house. "Where are you off to in such a hurry, missy?"

Brenna stuck her head out the open car window. "Papa, remember I told you I got a part-time job? Today's the day for the first meeting with Nicholas."

Ramon adjusted his suspenders and eyed her with a sharp intent. "You mean that fancy fellow over from San Antonio? Are you sure about working for some stranger?"

"Very sure." She cranked the car and waved at her perpetually perplexed father. "The pay is good, so I'll be able to help you with some rent money."

"Don't need no rent from my own daughter," Ramon said on a disgruntled huff, his south Louisiana accent thickening like a steaming roux.

They'd already had this argument. "I know that, but your daughter wants to contribute."

She blew him a kiss and took off before he insisted on escorting her. Papa was such a sweetheart. It was rather endearing how he watched over his three girls. But they all put up with it because they loved him and they all missed their mother, Lila. Especially Papa.

That strong thread of love kept Brenna going each day when she woke up in her old bed and stared at the aged pictures of her cheerleading days and the pictures of now-old rock stars she often dreamed about. Those still hung curled next to her prints of Van Gogh and Monet. She'd always loved sunflowers. She'd dreamed of going to Europe to explore all the places she'd only read about in art books. Maybe even get back into painting pictures herself.

So many dreams, and all for naught. She'd had to admit defeat and come back home. Who could paint that picture?

But at least she had a welcoming home and a solid foundation of faith to guide her. Jeffrey Patterson, her ex-fiancé, had frowned on such things. He didn't need anyone to "guide" him, as he'd often told her.

Now she had to wonder what she'd ever seen in the man. Maybe a bit of prestige and a way to penetrate the high-brow society of Baton Rouge? Now she realized she didn't need those things as much as she needed someone to love with authentic intent. And someone to love her back completely.

So when she pulled her car up the winding drive of Fleur House and saw Nicholas standing there in jeans and his own button-up shirt, she ignored the little dips and sways of her battered heart. The man cut a fine figure, there on the porch of the looming mansion.

Too fine.

Maybe she should turn around and go back to waiting tables.

Nick heard the car roaring up the drive. So she drove a late-model economy car that looked like a go-cart. Interesting. The car was cute in a strange kind of way and seemed to suit her. He watched as she climbed out and adjusted her briefcase strap over her shoulder. Even though she was dressed in casual clothes, she looked ready to be professional. He needed to be professional, too.

"Hello," he called as he moved down the rounded stone steps to meet her. "You're right on time."

She smiled and shook his hand. "I didn't want to be late."

Nick discreetly checked her fingers for an engagement ring. Her fingers were bare, but she wore a nice watch on one arm and a dainty flower-encrusted bracelet on the other. Sunflowers. Quaint and totally unexpected.

He let go of her hand, the memory of her slender fingers now burned into his mind. "I think you're already familiar with the layout of the house, but we can do a walk-through and I'll explain what I'd like to do. We've cleared away the debris and cobwebs and done most of the heavy renovations, but we kept some of the furniture the previous owner sold with the house."

She took a sweeping look at the brick-and-stone house. "Are you the decorator, too?"

"No, I have a designer coming from San Antonio to oversee that area. I'll mostly work on the structure and design of the house, preserving its history but improving it and bringing it up to speed, code-wise. The owner understands the historical significance of this place, but he requires the modern amenities, too."

Her gaze landed back on him. "And who is this mysterious owner?"

He held up his index finger and wagged it. "I'm not at liberty to say right now."

She gave him a questioning glance but didn't press. "All right, then. As long as his money is green, I'm good with that. Let's get on with the job."

Nick smiled and guided her up into an enclosed porch surrounded by an intricate stone facing that consisted of wide arches and then opened to the double front doors. "We've kept all of the fan transoms over the doors. Brings in a lot of light all over the house. Most of the windows have been replaced with more weatherproof glass, but we'll make sure we keep the hooded design."

"Wow." Brenna stood in the big open hallway and stared at the curving staircase. "This sure looks different. Last time Callie and I sneaked in here, it looked like cattle had run through the house."

"I wouldn't doubt that cows might have found shelter here along with a lot of other things," he said. "It was a mess."

"But it's gold underneath all that grim."

Nick knew this project would be his biggest challenge. "It is a work of art," he said. "But a true representation of a time gone by."

Even though the wallpaper had been aged and crumbling and the floors were scratched and rotted out in places, the house was striking.

Brenna seemed to see that, too. "It's just as beautiful as I remember—from peeking in the windows, even as run-down as it looked back then. I can't believe I get to help with the renovations. Callie loves this place more than I do. She's always dreamed of living here."

"Yes, she's mentioned that to me several times."

Nick enjoyed the blissful expression on Brenna's face. It took his breath away, but he held that breath so she wouldn't notice. But this attitude was new and refreshing. Most of the women he knew only wanted the house, not all the pain and work that would need to go into the house. They'd be bored with the details but more than willing to find someone to help them gut this house and make it what they thought it should be.

Brenna wanted it to be the same, only better.

That made her the perfect choice for helping him to find just the right pieces to complement the enormous walls and high ceilings throughout the place.

"Italianate Second Empire," she said on a sigh of appreciation. "Built in 1869 by a rich man from Paris who married a Creole woman from New Orleans. She named the town and the house. It's called Dubois House, after their last name, but the locals call it Fleur House. She did, too. I think because the gardens used to be full of all sorts of exotic plants and flowers."

"I'm impressed," Nick said. "And to think I had my doubts about hiring you."

She clutched her briefcase strap. "You did? But you said I'd be perfect."

Why did that little bit of uncertainty in her voice shake him to his core?

"I think you are." He tested her a bit more. "But we didn't exactly go through a formal interview."

"No, we met at a wedding. And didn't hit it off too well. And you hired me in a diner, after I'd waited on you with an attitude. I had my doubts, too."

He accepted that and bowed his head in agreement. "*Sí*. That makes us even."

"And…cautious."

He'd have to remember that.

"The parlor is to the right," he said, trying to stay on track. "And the dining room to the left."

She rushed into the huge square parlor, her flats making a nice cadence against the aged wooden floors. "Look at these windows—love those high arches. And that fireplace. I can just see some sort of outdoor scene surrounded by a gilded frame. Or better yet, a blue dog painting."

"Blue dog?" Nick chuckled. "You mean by George Rodrigue?"

"Yes, maybe something that bold and different would offset these amazing floor-to-ceiling windows."

She had that dreamy look on her face again. That look that made him want to sweep her into his arms and dance her around this big, empty room.

"I'll make a note—blue dog."

"Is he married?"

"Who?"

"Your boss?"

Nick snapped back to reality. "Uh, no. He was once, but his wife died."

She stopped smiling. "How awful. Our mother died several years ago. Breast cancer."

"I'm sorry. Callie did mention that. I can't imagine going through that. I still have both my parents and I'd be lost without them." He didn't tell her that he *had* lost a loved one, too. He knew the pain of grief, but he refused to open up that wound to someone he'd just met. "Your mother sounds like a special person."

She turned, her forest-colored eyes full of a richness that looked every bit as pretty as any picture he could imagine. "She was. You're blessed to have both of your parents. Enjoy them and love them."

"Good advice." He did love his family, but they'd grown apart over the years. Did he dare tell her that grief had stricken his family to the point of denial?

Better to focus on work.

He motioned toward the dining area. "Let's go to the other side."

Brenna let out a little squeal of delight, her smile lighting the room with an ethereal glow. "Look at that mural. Can we keep that?"

"Yes," he said, thinking he'd meant to do away with it. He'd have to tell the interior decorator that the elaborate rendition of a garden party with a steamboat in the background was off-limits.

Because he'd decided he didn't want to do anything that would take that beautiful smile off Brenna Blanchard's face.

And he'd also decided that he was in serious trouble.

Chapter Four

"Really?" Brenna smiled big at her new boss. "Just like that, you'll keep the mural?"

"I'm not always so agreeable," Nicholas said, giving her an exaggerated frown. "Your enthusiasm is obviously wearing off on me."

Brenna couldn't believe it was that easy. She'd prepared herself for a difficult task at every turn. "You seem like the type who bosses everyone around with a growl, waving your hand at this one and that one while you're on your phone with someone mysterious and even more demanding than you."

He actually laughed out loud.

And took her breath away.

"You've got me pegged, I see."

"I've worked with many highly demanding artists and supervisors," she said, her smile dying. "I miss that."

He motioned toward the stairs. "So you think you'll get bored with just me to growl at you?"

The thought of him actually doing that only added to the tremendous attraction she felt toward him. Bad, bad idea.

"No, I'm never bored. I always find something to do. But please, growl and be mean. Keeps me on my toes."

"I gave you the mural," he said after they reached the bottom of the stairs. "Make it beautiful for me."

Brenna did a slow swallow to get her breath under control. She got the distinct feeling this man didn't give anything easily. "I will," she said on a meek but firm tone. "And if I make everything else I choose beautiful for you, will that be a good thing?"

He put his hand on her back and urged her up the stairs. "That will be a very good thing. This house is the biggest renovation of my career. It's a make-or-break deal."

She whirled, one step above him, and stared down into his dark, rich-chocolate eyes. "And you picked me to help out. Are you loony?"

His eyes went even darker. "I've been called loco, *sí.*"

Brenna didn't think the man was crazy. No, rather she decided she was the loony one. Her impulsive nature always got her into trouble, but her sensible side usually tugged her back to earth. And even though she was standing on a centuries-old staircase looking down at a man who most certainly would make any woman swoon, no matter the time or place, she held herself aloof and told herself to snap out of it. She was here for a job not a new boyfriend.

"I've been called that, too," she said before turning away again. "We should get along just fine."

He did that growling thing. "Take a right on the landing."

"What are we looking at now?" she asked, afraid to glance back at him because she could feel the heat of his gaze following her. No, stalking her like a big cat out in the swamp.

He made it to the landing and looked around the wide, empty hallway. "This floor contains four bedrooms and baths for each. The baths were installed much later after the house was built, of course. We've finished the basic renovations, but we still have a lot of work to do up here. We enlarged the baths and the closets and made sure the structure is sound as far as wiring and knocking down walls. But your job is to pick one piece of interesting art for each room, especially the master bedroom."

"I'm on it," Brenna said, scribbling notes while she tried to ignore his sultry accent and his growling explanations. "Does your…mysterious owner have any preferences?"

"He has a few, but in this case, he told me to surprise him."

"Surprise. That's a new one. I like a good challenge." Brenna thought about that, then whirled. "Are you the owner, Nicholas?"

He backed away, hands out and pushing toward her. "I am not and that is the truth." He tugged her into a gigantic room with two sets of exquisite bay windows—obviously this was the master suite. "You see that trailer down there?"

Brenna nodded, ignoring the panoramic view of the Big Fleur Bayou and the bay out beyond for now. "Nice, but not quite as big as the house."

"That is my home," he said. "I renovate and design houses. But I prefer spending most of my time in my trailer or in a small hacienda on my parents' property in San Antonio. So I need you to understand—this is not my house. I have no desire to live here. I'm only here to prepare this estate for the new owner and then I'll move on to my next project."

She believed him. Nicholas didn't want to settle down. She got the message loud and clear. So she put aside her shock and awe and disappointment, then tried to throw him off by asking about the real owner. "Got it. You like to travel light and linger not so much. So back to the man who hired you. When will he arrive?"

He looked relieved and a bit shocked himself. "In the spring of next year. So we need to get busy."

He motioned to her with an impatient jabbing of his fingers in the air. Brenna turned away from the view outside to the reality of the man by her side. "Okay, so you're not the mysterious owner and you're not teasing me or trying to pull one over on me. I get that. So show me the rest of the house and give me the interior designer's phone number. I'll have to get with her and make sure I have a clear understanding of what she has planned."

He seemed to relax. Like a big cat, he'd almost pounced on her for being so nosy. But he'd pulled back, slinking away before he revealed anything too personal. "The designer knows she is to work with you in considering the art. Whatever you decide, she will work around it. Or make it work, per my instructions."

He once again reminded her of his authority.

But Brenna was known for always having the last word. "And just so we're clear, I'm only curious about the owner because I need to match the art to the person who will live here. But I have to say, Nick, you are every bit as mysterious as he-who-shall-not-be-mentioned-again. I'm sorry if I overstepped in being nosy. It's one of my flaws."

His dark eyebrows lifted. "Just one? You mean you have more?"

She saw that trace of a smile trying to pull at his lips. Saw that and so much that he didn't want her to see.

He didn't want to talk about the man who had bought Fleur House. But he especially didn't want to talk about himself, either. Which only made Brenna more curious.

Two hours later, Brenna waved goodbye to Nick and headed straight into town to her sister Alma's café. She needed comfort food and she needed some girl talk with Alma's right-hand woman and newly promoted manager, Winnie. And just to be sure, she called Callie, too. "I need to rant. Preferably over pie and coffee."

"Oh, I can't wait to hear all the details," Callie said. "I'll put Thelma at the front register and I'll be right over."

Brenna was about to disconnect but then she remembered. "Oh, Callie, Nick said he wants you to be in charge of all the landscaping once the house is done."

"Really?" Her sister squealed so loud Brenna had to hold her cell phone away. "I wanted to offer, but I chickened out and never applied. I dreamed about doing that, but I can't believe he actually asked for me. You didn't force him, did you?"

Brenna got an image of trying to force Nick Santiago into doing anything. Impossible. "Oh, no. He's not the kind to bend to the whims of a woman. He asked for you outright."

A brief memory of Nick telling her to make the mural beautiful fluttered through her mind. Okay, maybe he did bend to the whims of a woman every now and then.

Callie chatted on, excitement in every word. "Okay. I won't say anything until he brings it up. But I'll start playing with some garden designs. I know the layout of that acreage by heart, anyway."

"Yes, you've always wanted to live there and you've dreamed of cultivating that big garden. I know, I know. And after seeing the house, I can understand why. That's your thing, sis, not mine. I just get to help decorate the place."

She said goodbye, then again thought back over her sometimes-good, sometimes-bad conversation with Nick.

"Make it beautiful for me."

She'd seen the dare in his eyes when he'd said that. And she'd heard the gentleness in his request. Nick might not be the kind she could sweet-talk or force, but he could be the kind who would do something sweet and special simply because it pleased him. And he had done it for her, too, she sensed. But why? The man certainly presented a paradox. Too strange and spine-tingling for her to figure out right now, but too mysterious and intriguing for her to let go just yet.

"I'll need to read up on how to restore a mural," she said to get her mind off Nick and his "make it beautiful for me" lips. Then she pulled into a parking space across from the Fleur Café and hurried in to spill everything to Winnie and Callie.

Nick stood in the empty drawing room of Fleur House and sniffed the last of the sweet notes of Brenna's floral perfume. The smell of wisteria and jasmine hung in the air like a wedding veil, light and full of mystery.

And she thought he was the mysterious one.

He felt as empty as this big house.

Her laughter had echoed out over the quiet, still rooms like a rogue wind invading a hot house. Brenna seemed all buttoned-up and professional, but Nick thought there might be a free spirit hidden underneath that sensible facade. Did he dare encourage that side of her?

No, because he'd practically shouted at her to back off on trying to figure out what made him tick. He didn't have the right to encourage her in any aspect. He couldn't allow himself to get close to her, either. No time for that. He had to get this house in order and move on.

And where are you going?

The voice shouted into the silence of the afternoon and moved through the last of the sun's rays as he did one more walk-through of the house.

Tomorrow, the noise level would change and he wouldn't have to be alone with his silence. He'd be surrounded once again by hammers and drills and nail guns and saws. He'd hear the familiar sounds of workmen arguing and measuring, the noise of readjusting and tearing down. Demolition and restoration always signaled a change in the air, a forward movement of action. These were the sounds that soothed him. Not the laughter of a woman who seemed to be such a beautifully confusing contradiction. He'd smell the scent of sawdust and paint thinner, the scent of new paint and new wood, not the scent of wisteria and jasmine.

Tomorrow, he'd be in the thick of things again and then he could lose himself in his work, day and night.

Except for the times he'd lose himself in watching Brenna Blanchard making everything she touched beautiful.

He strolled toward the old mural that he'd saved after her last-minute plea. The genteel vista spoke of times gone by, times with smiling people walking along the bayou. The women wore colorful colliding frocks and the men looked dapper and distinguished in their waistcoats and top hats.

"Make it beautiful for me, Brenna," he said out loud, the echo of his solitude shouting back at him.

And he knew, she'd already made everything beautiful.

Too beautiful.

"He said that?" Winnie grabbed her coffee and took a long swig, her pecan-brown eyes going wide.

"He said exactly that," Brenna replied, her fork of bread pudding somewhere between her plate and her mouth. "And it was the way he said it, as if he'd never seen anything beautiful before."

"Must be some mural on that wall," Callie retorted through a mouthful of the creamy pudding. She finished chewing and let out a sigh. "It's so romantic."

"He is not romantic," Brenna said. "Didn't you hear the part about him living in a trailer and always being on the move? The man might as well wear a sign that says 'Don't bother. I ain't buying any.'"

"Or maybe the man protests too much," Winnie replied with her usual sweet smile. "And that in itself is highly romantic."

"He's not romantic," Brenna repeated, trying to convince herself. She couldn't do it, so she gave up. The man was like a walking Heathcliff—shuttered, disengaged, disturbing…and the total package, the kind of package a woman couldn't help but tear open. She wanted to dive right in and find the treasure. But she couldn't, wouldn't do that.

"I mean, the house is so romantic," Callie said with another sigh, completely ignoring Brenna's denial. "I hope I get to sneak in with you and see it all gussied up. I've always—"

"Wanted to live there," Brenna finished. "We all know that." She shrugged and shot her sister an indulging smile. "At least the new owner is single. He's a widower. You might have a chance."

"Oh, how tragic…and romantic," Callie said on another sigh. "At least we can understand how the man must feel. But why buy such a big house if he's all alone?" Her expression turned dreamy. "I know. He wants to wander around from room to room, lamenting his lost love. Tragic and poignant."

Brenna looked at her sister. "Have you ever considered writing a romance novel?"

Winnie brought some clarity to the situation. "Maybe he bought the house for his *new* bride."

Callie sat up straight, ignoring Brenna's question and Winnie's speculation. "I need to lose about ten pounds and do something about my sallow, washed-out skin and what about these laugh lines? What can I do about that?" She pushed at her long curly golden hair. "And maybe a haircut."

"No," both Winnie and Brenna said.

"Don't cut your hair," Brenna told her sister. "It took you a while to get it long again."

Callie nodded, quiet now. "You're right. I do have good hair in spite of losing it all...before. And besides, what am I thinking? Winnie might be right. He's probably found a new wife already. Of course, I don't want to fool with another man. Too much trouble. I might be in remission, but I'm still too tired to tackle a relationship."

"Amen," Brenna said. "I don't mind you stepping out, but not me. So I had a little talk with myself on the way over here. I will remain professional and businesslike. I won't pry into Nick's life at all."

"Yeah, right," her sister said. Then she leaned close. "Might want to test that theory. Nick just walked in the door and he's headed straight for our table."

Brenna gasped. "Why is it that all the men in our life always wind up in this café? Remember how Julien hounded Alma every day, over pie and petulance?"

Winnie giggled. "And suga', we sure got both."

Callie looked up with mock-surprise on her face. "Nick Santiago. How in the world are you?"

"Hello, ladies." Nick couldn't help the grin that smeared the sternness off his face. "As if you don't already know that I'm demanding, surly and hard to work with. I'm sure your pretty sister has filled you in on all my bad qualities."

Callie didn't take the bait. "Actually, I've been the one filling her in—on what a nice man you *can* be. I've sent enough flowers with your signature on them to know."

Nick really liked the Blanchard sisters, especially their somewhat sweet naïveté. "Sending flowers does not complete my résumé, Callie." He gave Brenna a direct stare.

Callie didn't let that stop her. "No, but I'm pretty good with getting it right with my regulars. You're the real deal, Nick."

Brenna cleared her throat. "This little mutual admiration society is endearing, but I have to get going. My boss *is* demanding." She shot Nick a daring smile. "Just passing through or did you need to speak to me?"

Nick wanted to keep sparring but duty called. "Actually, I wanted to see both you and Callie. And Winnie, too, for that matter."

Winnie slapped the table. "The highlight of my day, for true."

Brenna gave her sister a covert glance. "Have you changed your mind about hiring both of us?"

"No," Nick said, accepting the glass of water Winnie offered him. "I'm calling an impromptu meeting later this week. Kind of a town hall thing. I've had so many questions about what's happening with Fleur House, I thought I'd answer all of them in one fell swoop."

"Smart," Callie said. "What day and time?"

"Six-thirty Thursday, inside the church fellowship hall." He turned to Brenna. "And I want you there to take a few notes on ideas the people of Fleur might have about the house and gardens. We have a gem of a home right here in Fleur and my client wants to make sure everyone here is comfortable with what will probably become a tourist attraction. He hopes to open both the house and the gardens for tours at certain times when he's traveling on business."

"I'll be there," Brenna replied, touched that both Nick and he-who-she-couldn't-mention were willing to do this for the town.

Callie stood up. "Nick, you have to tell us about this man."

Nick shook his head. "I can't do that. My contract has a very precise confidentiality clause."

"Which we will honor," Brenna replied, sending her sister a warning look.

"Oh, all right." Callie made a face. "Want a bowl of bread pudding, Nick?"

Nick glanced at Brenna. "I shouldn't—"

"Oh, live a little, boss," Brenna said. "It might make you sweeter."

He laughed at that. "I'll have some, then. With

some of that strong coffee Fleur seems to be famous for."

Callie brought him his pudding and coffee. "I have to get back to work. I'll see y'all later."

He watched as Brenna gathered her things, obviously in a hurry to get away from him. "What is this? I have to eat all alone?"

She stopped, glanced around. "I see a lot of people in here."

"I don't know them yet."

"You don't know me yet, either," she said. "I'll be at your meeting and I'll take copious notes, but right now I want to research some art for the house. I want to get this right as much as you do, believe it or not."

"I believe you," he said, wishing she'd stay while he willed her to go. "Go, get to work. I am paying you a lot of money, after all."

"Yes, sir."

He watched her walk away, that elusive fragrance following her. Then he looked up to find Winnie smiling down at him.

"I'm still here," she said with a grin.

Nick laughed at that because he was pretty sure Winnie was married and had four children. "Sit down and keep me company, then. And while you're at it, maybe you can tell me why I find that woman so fascinating."

Chapter Five

Brenna sat watching the people of Fleur as they filed into the bright church hall one by one. Of course, Winnie had sent cookies to go with the urn of coffee. Refreshments were always a requirement here in this big, loud room. The Fleur Café, right across the street, was happy to provide them.

Good thing she brought extra. Tonight the main attraction had drawn a record crowd. Whenever a stranger came to town and wanted a meeting, people came to listen. Especially people who were unemployed or late with last month's mortgage. Especially people who already had two and sometimes three jobs but could never rest because their families needed food and shelter. Not that Nick came bearing jobs or solutions, but he was here on a positive note. He was taking something they all treasured and admired and making it beautiful again.

A restoration.

Brenna let that thought rush through her like sparkling water as she scanned the crowd. Nick wasn't here yet. Why was she so nervous, so hopeful for this man? What had he done to her to make her see beneath that facade of cool and calm he cloaked around himself?

"Make it beautiful for me."

His words echoed over the boisterous gathering, haunting her with a sweet intensity.

Did Nick create and re-create lovely aesthetic things because he needed to make the world more beautiful? For someone he loved? Or maybe for someone he'd lost? Was that why he traveled so light and lingered only as long as required? She thought about the young girl in the portrait she'd seen on the internet. What did Jessica mean to him? Was she a friend? Or someone he'd loved and lost?

Dear Lord, help me to understand this man. Help me to restore his soul to You.

The plea of that prayer poured over her as people gathered for the meeting. And somehow, Brenna knew that would be the echo she'd hear in her head each time she was around Nick Santiago.

For now, she smiled and waved to the full house. She spotted Julien's younger brother, Pierre, along with his girlfriend, Mollie. They were so cute together. Since Julien and Alma had gotten back together, the Blanchard family had embraced Julien's family, welcoming his mother and his brother as their own. Her father came through the door, Mrs. LeBlanc walking with him. It was funny how several of the widows in the church seemed to be always after her daddy. But Julien's mother was just a friend. She had made it clear after her husband died almost two years ago she would never fall in love again.

Maybe Nick had made that same pledge, Brenna thought as she surveyed the crowd.

Callie came in and waved, then slid into a seat up front.

Brenna walked over to her sister and dropped her briefcase on the floor. "He's not here yet."

"I'm sure he's on his way," Callie said. "Hey, I got a call from Alma. They are having so much fun. The ocean, the beach, the shops, the honeymoon. She might not ever come home from Florida."

"She's in love," Brenna said, glad for her sister. "Did you tell her about Fleur House?"

Callie giggled. "Yes, I told her all about your new love interest Nick Santiago, which is what you're really asking."

"I am not. What did she say?"

"She said good for you. On the job…and the man."

"She's in love. She can be optimistic."

"Yeah, that's true. We, on the other hand, are more cynical. So we have to be cautious."

Brenna nodded at that, as sad as it sounded. But when she turned and saw Nick strolling in as if he owned the place, his suit tailored and fitted, his hair combed and shimmering, she wanted to throw caution to the wind. Her heart actually did a backward flip.

Frances LaBorde, a staunch church lady and one to always notice everything going on around here, leaned up and touched Brenna on the arm. "He's mighty perty, ain't he?" She winked at Brenna, then settled back with a look of delight on her puffy cheeks.

"Yes, he sure is," Callie whispered to Brenna. "If you don't go for him, I just might have to."

"Go ahead," Brenna said, inhaling a deep breath. "Ours is a working relationship." She ignored the little green monsters of jealousy laughing in her head.

"Yeah, and we all believe that," Callie retorted. "I was just teasing about my going after him. But the way he looks at you, I think you have a definite shot."

Nick surveyed the crowd. The tough crowd. He hadn't expected this many people to show up. But this was a small town with a big grapevine. No need for online networking here. This network moved through clotheslines and crab traps and church prayer chains.

He was a stranger in a strange land.

Then he looked up and saw Brenna sitting there on the front row, prim and proper and prepared, wearing a pretty spring dress and cute little blue sweater. She gave him an encouraging, questioning smile.

Showtime.

"Hello, everyone," he said in a loud calm voice.

The whispers died down as people settled into their seats.

Nick took a breath. "I'm Nick Santiago. I've been here for a while, but I've been so busy I haven't had time to talk to very many of you. I'm supervising the renovation of the Dubois mansion, locally known as Fleur House."

Applause followed that introduction. Nick grinned at that.

"I wanted to let you know what this means for your community."

"Yeah, what does it mean?" came a shout from the back.

"Jobs?" someone else asked.

The conversations started up again, a mixture of English and Cajun-French that turned into chaos. Nick tried raising his hand, but they were off and running, taking his initial explanations and creating little detours that rippled like a swamp wake.

"Excuse me!"

Nick watched as Brenna stood up and clapped her hands.

"Mr. Santiago is doing us a favor by bringing us here tonight. Let's show him that famous Fleur hospitality by *listening,* please. He'll be glad to answer any questions when he's finished."

The room went quiet.

Nick gave Brenna a grateful glance, then started again.

"Last spring, my client bought Fleur House and the surrounding gardens. Because I'm an architect and on retainer for this particular client, he commissioned me to oversee the renovations. I've been here a few weeks now, and I've seen some of you riding by the house. I know you're wondering who this man is and what's going on with all the construction."

He took a breath and drank a sip of water from the cup Brenna had put on a table. "I can't tell you who the owner is yet. He's a very private man with a very public obligation. But I can tell you about me. I grew up in San Antonio, Texas. My parents still live there." He stopped, glanced at Brenna, prayed she wouldn't see his doubts. "I've always loved old buildings. That is my specialty, restoring old neglected places and making them new again."

"We're glad to have you."

Nick nodded at the robust man who'd shouted

that out. "And I'm glad to be here. So we will get serious about putting the final touches on the house now that the toughest parts of the renovation are finished. I've hired Brenna Blanchard to oversee some of the decor for the house, mainly the artwork. My client loves art and buys several pieces a year. Brenna will pick some of the main pieces for the house." He glanced at Brenna and smiled. "She is highly qualified."

"And she's an artist, too," someone called out.

Surprised, Nick took another sip of water. "Really? She left that off her résumé."

While Brenna shifted in her seat and looked down, another person said, "She don't like to brag."

Everyone laughed at that. But Nick made a note to ask Brenna about her hidden talent. Was it coincidence that she was also an artist? Did he dare tell her he used to paint? That was a lifetime ago. It didn't matter much now.

"So, what other talents do we have in this room? We're a little behind on the renovations, so I need some extra hands. I'll need some extra construction workers—both experienced and nonexperienced. I'll need a couple more electricians and plumbers, and journeymen to add to my team. I'll need a qualified house inspector. I have a list of positions here on the table. Please feel free to take the information. Even though I have a team from Texas, I'll still need a lot of locals to help. I'll be back here tomorrow at noon to accept applications. Mainly, I'm here to make Fleur House fresh and new again so that we can show it off to the community and to tourists and visitors, too."

Everyone clapped, then Brenna stood up. "Now, if you have any questions—"

An hour later, Brenna shooed the last person out the door, then turned to Nick. "Welcome to Fleur."

He ran a hand over his hair and laughed. "I'm exhausted."

He did look adorably exhausted. She had to keep her fingers from brushing through his dark hair. "And hungry, I imagine."

"Yes, I am." He started gathering his notes and shoved them into his briefcase. "I didn't realize that until now, however."

Brenna waffled like a frog on a vine, then finally turned to him. "You're invited to my daddy's house for chicken perlo. It's my mama's recipe, but Papa has perfected it. It's always good on a crisp fall night."

"That sounds great." He touched her midback and guided her toward the door. "How did I do?"

Brenna didn't have to hide her reaction to that. "You were great. I had no idea you'd be able to offer people jobs. I guess I never asked."

She'd been too concerned about herself even

to think of that. Once she'd been hired, she did her usual thing. She began to obsess about being perfect.

He gave her an indulgent smile. "I have my own crew, but we always try to hire locals and now that we're down to the wire, it makes sense. I should have explained that to you."

Interesting. "So you do this a lot. Find a house, renovate it and move on?"

"*Sí.* That's my job. My client keeps me busy year-round. He's mostly into industrial real estate, but he sometimes buys estates and renovates them. He's bought and sold some incredible homes."

More and more information. But she wanted to know more about Nick right now. "Is he your main employer?"

Nick held the door for her. Outside, the fall night held a hint of winter. While the winters here were mild, it was beginning to be chilly enough to wear a light jacket.

Brenna only had a light sweater. She shivered.

"I work for several different people, but mostly for him, *sí.*"

And that was the end of that.

She shivered again. Then she felt Nick's hands on her arms, felt the warmth of his soft wool suit jacket enveloping her shoulders. "You're cold."

And you are seriously…hot.

Brenna reeled in her treacherous reaction, the

scent of soap and spice all around her. "Thank you. I have to remember to unpack my winter clothes."

"Do you need a ride?" he asked. Then he motioned to his car. Only she'd never seen a car like this one.

"What...what is that exactly?"

He grinned like a schoolboy. "That is a vintage 1969 GTO convertible with four-on-the-floor and a 400 horsepower engine with a turbo transmission."

Brenna looked at the baby blue automobile, then back at him. "A muscle car? You drive a muscle car?"

He looked surprised. "You know about muscle cars?"

"I've heard my papa and Julien and his brother, Pierre, talking about them, usually when they're watching a race on television. And now I've actually seen one."

He took her by the arm. "Not only seen one, but get to ride in one."

Brenna glanced around, then realized her father had left her! "I guess I do. I came with my daddy, but apparently both he and my sister forgot about me." On purpose, no doubt.

"Not a problem," he said, hurrying around to open the passenger-side door for her. "I would get lost without you."

Did the man realize he had a way with words? Did he even know that the way he said things with that exquisite hint of an accent went right to a woman's heart?

She could speak one thing and mean another, too. "I don't want you to get lost."

His dark eyes gleamed like midnight water. "Then let's go.

"Top down?"

She nodded. She needed the cold wind to make her snap out of this massive crush.

With that, he got in and cranked the motor. The car purred like a great cat. Nick shifted gears and Brenna held on for dear life, her breath caught in the cool night air. This man with all his fancy things had first reminded her of Jeffrey. But Nick Santiago was nothing like her shallow, self-centered, very ex-fiancé. As Callie had said, he seemed to be the real thing.

At least he felt real, driving this powerful machine, his hands only inches away from her. Brenna tried to focus on breathing. He was too close, way too close.

"Where am I going?" he asked.

Brenna came out of the fog surrounding her mind. "Oh, take a left at the next traffic light. Our house is a few miles out of town, on the Big Fleur Bayou. When you see the sign for Blanchard's Landing, you're there."

"What is chicken perlo?" he asked, grinning over at her.

"Well, it's chicken and rice and spices and we serve it with corn bread and biscuits, all home-made. It's usually cooked in a big iron pot."

He hit a hand on the steering wheel. "The food down here is so good."

Brenna couldn't deny that. "But I've been to San Antonio. The food there is wonderful, too."

"Yes, and my mom is a good cook."

She wanted to know all about his family. "So you're an only child?"

He slowed the car as they reached the sign she'd mentioned, then turned into the next driveway.

"Yes." He parked the car in the long driveway leading to the white cottage and stared into the darkness. "I have been for a long time now. But I had a sister. She died when I was a teenager."

Shock hit at Brenna with the ticking of the car's cooling engine. She thought about the girl in the painting. "I'm so sorry. What happened?"

"It's complicated," he said. Then he got out and came around to open her door.

"I didn't mean to pry," Brenna said. "I'm sorry."

Nick stared down at her, his eyes shimmering dark in the moonlight over the bayou water. "It's okay. One day, I'll explain. But for now, I'd rather not discuss it."

"Then we won't." She took his hand, needing to show him some sort of comfort. "Let's go inside."

He nodded and remained quiet. But he didn't let go of her hand.

Chapter Six

Warmth enveloped Nick when he stepped inside the quaint cottage on the bayou. The house was bigger than it looked from the road. It went back a long way, starting with a big living room that led into an even bigger kitchen where paned windows and a set of French doors led to a big porch and an open view to the bayou beyond. Out on the boathouse and dock, white lights twinkled like fireflies in the night.

"Amazing," he said to Brenna as she called out to her father. "This is a nice house."

She smiled and handed him his coat back. "It's not Fleur House, but my papa built it with his own hands—and help from a lot of people, too. It started out small and grew with each daughter. Papa decided long ago that we all needed our own space."

Nick laughed at that. "So he just kept adding rooms?"

"All da way out to da water," Ramon Blanchard called from the kitchen. "Plum ran out of land."

Brenna pulled Nick toward the long white-tiled kitchen counter. "Then he built a boathouse. We loved sleeping out there when we were growing up."

"Dat was fer your mama," Mr. Blanchard said. "She loved to sit out dere and read her 'woman novels' as she called dem." He threw his dish towel over his shoulder and held out his beefy hand to Nick. "Welcome. C'mon on in. We got plenty and den some."

Nick laughed while he caught up with Mr. Blanchard's heavy Cajun accent, then took the glass of sweet tea Callie handed him. "It sure smells great. Thanks for inviting me, Mr. Blanchard."

"It's Ramon. But most call me Papa."

"He's also Papa Noel at Christmastime," Callie said.

"I'll keep that in mind and try to stay off the naughty list," Nick replied. His gaze settled on Brenna. Her smile was small, but he caught the hint of dare in her eyes.

Mr. Blanchard's nod and mock-mean look made Nick think he might have to really be careful. A father always protected his daughters. Just the way his father had tried to protect his sister.

Callie tugged him toward the big long dining

table between the kitchen and the den. "Don't look so afraid. His bark is much worse than his bite."

Brenna nodded on that. "And he forgives all us at Christmas and Easter."

Ramon let out a grunt. "It is my burden to bear, having three lovely daughters. I have to forgive and forget most every day of the week."

"And you love it," Brenna said, kissing her father on the cheek. "Now let's eat. I'm starving."

Nick waited for the women to sit, then pulled out a chair. "This table is like a work of art. Did you build it, Ramon?"

"*Oui*. It's pure cypress. Built it for my own *mère* about fifty years ago. My papa and me, we built it together."

Nick admired the worn patina on the aged cypress planks of the long table. He imagined a lot of meals served on this mellow, dented wood. "You could feed an army on this thing."

"I've done dat, for sure," Ramon said with a belly-roll laugh. "Tonight, just us chickens."

The dinner progressed with good food and tall tales. The more Ramon Blanchard talked the more pronounced his Cajun-French became.

Brenna leaned close. "I'll have to explain most of that to you later."

Nick nodded and buttered another fat, flaky biscuit. Then he glanced over at the big stone fireplace on the long wall past the open counter. "Is that your mother?" he asked Brenna, nodding toward the portrait over the mantel of a beautiful blonde woman. She sat in a garden with the bayou behind her and cypress trees sheltering her.

"Yes," she said, the one word quieting the room. "Lila."

"Daughter Number Three painted that picture," Ramon said, his tone reverent and low but full of pride. "Bree always wanted to paint pretty pictures."

Nick shot Brenna a quick glance. "I heard someone mention that at the meeting. You didn't tell me that."

"I studied art," she said with a shrug. "Dabbling is a part of the procedure." She gave him another daring look.

"That is more than dabbling," Nick said, remembering how much he had once loved art, how he had once fancied himself an artist. He'd channeled that notion into creating and re-creating houses instead. But Brenna clearly had talent. "It's impressive."

She looked embarrassed, but her smile hid her obvious doubts. "Thank you. I am glad I painted our mother. It makes things easier now."

Everyone went quiet for a minute while Nick admired the portrait.

She'd captured the playfulness in her mother's face that spoke of the same spirit he'd seen in

Callie and Brenna. He imagined Alma had some of it, too. But where Alma had darker hair and a petite frame, Callie was tall and blond, more like her mother. And Brenna seemed to possess some of both parents. A nice mix. An interesting mix.

A dangerous mix.

"More chicken and rice?" Callie asked, her knowing gaze trapping him.

"Yes." Nick took the big bowl and dipped more of the seasoned rice and tender chicken. "This is really good."

Brenna took a sip of her tea. "We have sweet potato pie for dessert."

Nick moaned. "After three biscuits, I'd better skip the pie."

"You can't do dat," Ramon said, his frown like a broken boat. "Dis pie makes people sweet. You gonna need to be sweet dealing with Daughter Number Three, trust me."

Nick laughed at that. "Maybe you're right."

He took the pie. And ate every bite.

An hour later, after they'd done the dishes, Ramon decided it was time for him to retire and Callie said she needed to get back to her own house.

Brenna watched her sister go, a look of dread mixed in with her smile. Did she not want to be alone with him? Then she turned to Nick. "Want to sit awhile?"

He checked his watch. He had a big day tomorrow and a lot of work waiting tonight. But he didn't want to leave yet.

"For a few minutes." He followed her to the big plaid sofa across from the massive hearth. "You must love coming home to this place every day."

Brenna glanced around. "I do, but I didn't like having to move back in. I love my papa, but I enjoyed being independent and out on my own." She shrugged. "I always wanted to move away from Fleur. So did Alma, but now she's changed that tune. She and Julien plan to build a house in a few years. For now, they'll be living in our *grandmère's* cottage behind Fleur Café. Alma loves that old place. I think after they build the house, she hopes to turn it into a tea room—an extension of the café but more private—for luncheons and parties."

Nick took in all the informal information she offered. "I have to say the Blanchard sisters are an enterprising bunch. And you? You wanted the big city and art? Do you still paint?"

She seemed to squirm a bit. "Not for a long time. Jeffrey—that's my ex-fiancé—convinced me that I couldn't be a good curator if I spent too much time working on my own art." She stopped, took a long sigh. "He was critical of everything I painted, so I just—"

"Gave up?" Nick wanted to throttle this Jeffrey person. But he'd given up on a lot of things himself. Being around Brenna made him wonder if he needed to go back and change some of that.

"Yes." She glanced up at her mother's portrait. "But, hey, I have more time on my hands now. Maybe I'll pick it back up. I want to paint Callie. She's the most expressive one in the bunch."

Nick got up to study the portrait. "I think you should. And you should never let anyone else talk you out of your dreams."

"Good advice," she said. "I didn't have enough confidence to fight him. I think being with him stripped me of a lot of myself, if that makes sense."

Nick nodded. "Makes perfect sense. But why did you allow that to happen?"

She looked down at her hands. "I thought if I acted the way he thought I should act, he'd love me. Isn't that the craziest notion? I was taught all about unconditional love, but I never felt that with Jeffrey. I had this image of what type of man I wanted to marry in my mind. He fit the image— on paper, but not in reality. I messed up big-time."

He turned to stare down at her, marveling at how open and honest she seemed. "And now?"

Brenna got up. "Now, I'm home and I'm safe and I might try my hand at painting again. I intend to find myself again."

"I like hearing that." He picked up his suit coat. "You know, the light in the sunroom at Fleur

House lends itself to a painter's brush. Feel free to try it out—that is when the workers aren't milling around. We take Sundays off. That can be your time if you want it."

She looked shocked and grateful. "That's thoughtful of you, Nick."

"I can be thoughtful every now and then."

She smiled and walked him to the door. "Oh, that made me think about the mural. I've already called an expert I know in New Orleans. He's good at what he does, but expensive. I wanted to run that by you before I have him drive down."

"Money isn't an issue," Nick said. "Bring in your expert, bring in whatever experts you might need."

"Wow, an unlimited budget?"

"I didn't say that, but this is an estate renovation. We want everything to look rich but viewable. My client will probably sell it after a while, anyway. He travels too much to stay in one place."

"Same as you," she said, her hand on the door-knob.

Nick had lain down the law on how he liked to live, so he didn't try to deny it. "I hope I wasn't rude about that. People don't always understand." He shrugged. "And it's hard for me to explain."

"You're right, I don't understand," she said when they walked out onto the long, wide porch.

"You seem to love working on homes. Why don't you have one?"

It was a valid question.

So he tried to give her a truthful answer. "I left home at an early age and just kept on moving. After a few years of hotel rooms, the construction trailer just seemed like a good idea. I've never thought much about that. Until now."

She stared up at him, her golden-green eyes questioning and confused. "I didn't think I ever wanted to come back to Fleur. Until now."

Nick didn't know what to say. "I think we're both at a crossroad." And his seemed to be leading straight to her.

She leaned against a thick column. "Yes, I guess so. We'll see what happens, which way we both go."

A thick silence hung between them like a low, moss-draped cypress branch hanging over dark water.

"I enjoyed supper," he said, using the term her father had used. "I hope I can repay the favor one day."

"I enjoyed riding in that souped-up car," she replied. "Now go. I can tell you're eager to get to work."

"You know me already." Nick took her hand, held it there between them. "I'll see you tomorrow."

"Yes. Bright and early." She pulled away.

He wanted to bring her back. But then, she might get the impression that he wanted more.

And Nick wasn't sure he could give her more.

So he got in his car and cranked the engine.

When he turned to wave, she had already gone in the house.

Brenna woke early the next morning. She had not slept much, but she couldn't wait to get on with her new assignment. After the restraints of her job back in Baton Rouge and the constraints of trying to please Jeffrey, she felt a sense of relief in being able to try her hand at finding art for Fleur House. It would be a challenge, but it would also release all of her creative intuitions and give her days purpose.

"Mama always said we'd find our joy in our purpose," she replied to her reflection in the mirror.

She intended to do just that. She'd spent hours last night after Nick had left searching for information on Fleur House, both online and in a few of the history books her mother had loved. She was as prepared as possible for now. So she checked her white sweater and navy-blue full skirt, then threw on a strand of silver pearls and tugged on her dark gray knee-high boots. A light plaid jacket completed her look. Not too prissy but professional enough. Once she'd found all the pieces, she'd dress more casual for the installations. But she had a lot to do before that time came.

After a quick breakfast of fruit and toast, she called the mural expert in New Orleans and made arrangements for him to come to the house and see what he could do to restore the wall in the dining room. Then she printed out copies of various pieces of art, hoping to make some auction bids when the pieces were available.

She'd need to get the computer-generated charts of each room in the house so she could play with where to place each piece. Even though this was challenging, it reminded her of when she and her sisters had played with paper dolls.

Brenna smiled at the memory. Even back then, she would paint over the doll clothes to make them look better and more to her liking, which only infuriated her sisters. But Alma would cook imaginary food for the paper figures and of course, Callie would pick flowers to lay around the feet of the wobbly, thin pretend people. Funny how they all did the same things now but with real intentions and talents.

Yes, this was the real deal, Brenna reminded herself. And what a house! What a great blank canvas. She really did like this job and she liked Nick, too. A lot.

Work, Brenna. Work.

She thanked God for the opportunity and in the

same prayer, asked Him to give her the strength to focus on work.

And not on the man who'd hired her.

Nick heard saws grinding through wood. After going over the blueprints with the project foreman, he pulled on his jacket and hard hat and went out onto the wide front lawn of the property. From this spot, he had a good view of the front of the house.

The Italianate design boasted oval arches on the many balconies and porches and open arches surrounding the side portico which used to be the carriage driveway. This same pattern carried to the garages and outbuildings. He'd taken many pictures of the house, from all angles. But this morning, in the sunlight coming through the pines and old oaks, the house looked alive and glowing.

"It's smiling at us."

Nick turned to find Brenna standing a few feet away, looking all buttoned-up but ready to work.

"You think so?" he asked, motioning her from the shell-encrusted driveway to the cushiony grass.

"I'd be excited if I were getting a massive make-over," she said. Her high-heeled boots seemed to sink into the grass but she managed to make her way to him. She let out a sigh of contentment. "Even with all the flowers just about gone, this place is still beautiful." She pointed to the camellia bushes scattered through the yard. "I've tried to count those so I'll know if your men destroyed any of them."

"Oh, you want the camellia bushes to stay?"

"Not me," she said on a grin. "Callie made me promise to tell you that. She really has counted them and she knows the names of each variety—those funny scientific names. You have your winter camellias and your spring camellias and Callie loves all of them. Especially because they are 'old grown' as she likes to call them. She believes trees and bushes and blossoms can tell us stories if we listen."

Nick liked hearing about Callie and knew she'd make a great landscape director, but he especially loved listening to her sister talk—about anything at all. Brenna's accent was part Southern and part Cajun which made it endearing and enchanting.

"I love listening to your stories," he said. Then to clear up any misunderstandings, he added, "Your dad is a hoot. He has some good stories of his own."

"And spun with a few embellishments," she replied, her eyes ripe with an emotion Nick couldn't pinpoint. "We all do, I suppose."

Nick sensed she wanted to get to work. "Okay, so for now, you need to get to know the house, room by room. You have free rein, but if you are anywhere near construction, you need to wear a hard hat. Understood?"

"Yes, sir." Her burnished hair lifted in the chilly morning wind. "I thought I'd make some sketches of the focus walls in each room. And if you can give me notes and swatches on your paint samples and explain the overall style of the house, I'll have a better idea of what we're doing here."

Nick took her by the elbow. "We'll talk more about the overall theme of the renovations at lunch. I can show you the blueprints, too. I have those in my trailer."

She glanced up at him, her eyes going wide. "I'm anxious to see this famous trailer."

"It's not much, but it's home."

That statement hit him like the wind moving through the trees. He didn't really have a true home. Strolling across the lawn with Brenna, he wondered for the first time since he'd arrived in Fleur if maybe it was time for him to settle down and find one.

Chapter Seven

Nick's trailer was one part messy construction office and one part plush home away from home. It consisted of a big office filled with books and ledgers and pictures of the current project and a long desk covered with blueprints, notes and an open laptop.

Brenna glanced past the efficiency kitchen with the coffeepot and a big bowl of power bars and fruit to the combination sitting room/bedroom on the back side of the long building. The bedspread had been messily thrown toward the big pillows and the tiny room looked neat enough if she ignored the suit hanging on the door. She noticed coffee-table books on design and architecture stacked three feet high beside the bed. So Nick liked to do his homework, too. Set against the books, a picture of a beautiful dark-haired little girl caught her attention, reminding her of the portrait she'd found. His sister? Curiosity usually got Brenna in trouble, so she had to squelch the urge to dig deeper.

Turning to face him, she said, "I love what you've done with the place."

Nick grinned then offered her a chair. The only clear chair apparently. "I'm not always this messy. Things get crazy once a project gets going."

"I can organize things for you," Brenna offered. "I'm good at that kind of thing."

He glanced around, then back at her. "Not a good idea. My foreman might flip out. He's the messy one, but it's kind of a system he has and it works for him. So, thanks, but no thanks."

Brenna sank down and tried to put the idea of a clean work environment out of her mind, right along with the image of Nick in jeans and a heavy canvas jacket and hard hat. Time to get down to business. "I think the best thing I can do for now is take it room by room on the art. I'll match the proportions by the size and scope of the rooms. I already have some ideas for the entryway and the upstairs landing."

Nick nodded, then cranked up the laptop. "Let's look at the model rooms. That way you can also see the color swatches for each room. I'll give you a thumb-drive so you'll have everything you see here."

"I had a note to ask you about that. I used computer models to set up exhibits at the museum, so I'm picturing this as a really big museum."

He motioned for her to roll her chair over close to his desk. "Not a problem. I've been working on this for six months now, so I know the rooms in and out."

Brenna wasn't surprised. Pulling out her electronic pad, she said, "It takes a lot of work to do something of this size and scope. I hope I don't disappoint you."

His dark-eyed gaze held her. "Why would you think that?"

Brenna thought it was obvious. "I've never done anything like this. A five-thousand-square-foot estate house at that, and for a mysterious owner who refuses to show his face. It's a challenge."

His gaze danced over her face. "You'll be fine. Your eyes light up whenever you start talking about this house."

She wasn't so sure. "Why do you believe in me, Nick?"

He grinned at that. "Because of that spark I see in your eyes. And both of your sisters recommended you."

"Wow." Brenna didn't know why that should bring tears to her eyes but it did. "My family has always supported my efforts."

"They believe in you, so you need to believe in yourself."

Touched, Brenna decided to be positive. Other than her papa, she'd never had a man encourage her in the way Nick had. Was that part of being the boss, or did he see something in her she wasn't even aware of herself? "Okay, enough about my concerns. I'm excited and I want this to work."

He gave her a look that seemed to say the same thing, but not exactly about this house and her professionalism. His eyes, so dark and mysterious, reminded her of the blackest bayou waters. She saw secrets there, but she was afraid to find out about those secrets. She'd let Jeffrey roll right along without being honest and that had only brought her heartache. Did she hide her head in the sand when it came to men?

Glancing toward the stack of books by his bed, she told herself this time, she would stick to the business side of things and keep her heart out of this.

"Any other questions?" Nick asked, his gaze moving over the computer screen before he looked up at her.

They sat staring at each other for a long minute, but Brenna still didn't have the answers she needed. Reminding herself about work and not obsessing over this man and his past, she looked down at her notes. "I think I'm ready, boss."

"Okay, then. Let's get on with things."

Over the next hour, Nick showed her the computer-generated models of the house, room by room, including theme and colors and a mock-up of furnishings. When he stopped to take a phone call, Brenna took more notes as the ideas poured into her head. She was involved in the work ahead, but she couldn't forget the scent of leather mixed with sawdust that surrounded Nick and this place. Nor could she forget the forlorn theme that echoed out over the tiny trailer, especially whenever she glanced toward that picture of the pretty dark-haired little girl.

Figuring Nick would tell her about his sister if he wanted her to know, Brenna started imagining things. Obviously, his sister had died and obviously, it had affected Nick in a strong way. Was he running from his grief?

This trailer spoke of a life on the run, a life unsettled and unstoppable. Why couldn't Nick stop and find some rest? Was he running from something or did he enjoy his work to the point of ignoring life?

Could she help him with that? Or should she stay clear of getting tangled with yet another career-focused man?

He hung up, then turned to her. "The designer is driving over from San Antonio for a couple of days, probably next week. You'll be working closely with Serena."

Brenna didn't know why, but she didn't like the

idea of that. She'd left messages at the number Nick had given her, but had yet to hear from the mysterious Serena. "She's coming here?"

Nick smiled. "The interior designer I mentioned, yes. Serena Delrio. Top-of-the-line and very sought-after in Houston, Dallas and San Antonio."

Brenna suddenly felt small and insecure. "Sounds wonderful. What if I can't keep up?"

"Brenna, you'll work *with* her. Not for her."

"Of course." She snapped to and stood up. "It's just with an exotic name like that, she has to be… pretty and powerful, maybe hard to deal with."

He laughed. "You got all of that just from her name?"

"I'm imagining things," she replied. "I'm still nervous about the whole art and design thing. But it'll be good to work with an expert even though she's so busy she hasn't returned my calls."

"She's a beauty and yes, she stays busy," he readily admitted. "But bear with her. She'll get around to us in time. We've know each other for a long time. And yes, she can be a pistol, but I'm pretty sure you can handle her."

"Hmm." She let that filter through the haze of curiosity covering her brain. "This should be interesting."

He gave her a look that told her way more than words. "Oh, yes." Then he grabbed two hard hats. "C'mon, let's see what the crew's done in the kitchen this morning."

Brenna couldn't miss the excitement in his words. "You love this, don't you?"

He nodded, pushed a bright yellow hat on her head. "*Sí*. It's what I do. Why wouldn't I love it?"

Brenna didn't answer that rhetorical question. She didn't have to. This wasn't just his livelihood. This was his life.

And she didn't see much room in that life for anyone else.

Especially her.

"Serena. Even her name sounds beautiful."

Callie stopped walking down the long, wide middle aisle of Callie's Corner, her garden and landscaping nursery, and stared across at Brenna. "You have a nice name and you're cute."

Brenna gritted her teeth. She'd worked with Nick all last week and she'd gone back to Fleur House over the weekend. They'd talked a lot, laughed a lot and discussed the house from every aspect and angle. Now she had to worry about the next step in the process. "Cute won't cut it with someone who answers to the name Serena. She won't return my phone calls. I think I'm in over my head."

Elvis, the huge mutt of a dog her sister had taken in after her divorce, came traipsing up the aisle toward them, his big fluffy tail hitting at colorful mums and sweeping palm fronds. He woofed a hello at Brenna.

"Hello, you big baby," she said, holding him away. "Elvis, love me tender and don't mess up my clothes, okay?" Leaning over to pet the woolly dog, she glanced up at Callie. "Well, what do you think?"

Callie gave her a twisted smile. "I think you need to grow a backbone. It's not like you to cower in terror. You don't even know this person yet. Why borrow trouble?"

Brenna stood back up, dog hair on her hands and skirt. Elvis woofed again, clearly not finished saying hello. When the dog tried to jump up on her again, his wet paws inches from her shirt, Brenna held him away. "Elvis, go play in the fish pond and relive *Blue Hawaii*."

He glanced at her, tongue wagging, glanced at Callie then dropped and took off toward the back of the vast property.

Callie's frown didn't quite meet her eyes. "Great. He chases the koi. I've told you that."

"And he never actually goes all the way into the water," Brenna replied. "Maybe I'm like Elvis. I just enjoy staying on the edge, safe and secure."

Callie actually snorted. "You seriously need to dive right in and do the job you were hired to do. You always panic about things you're not sure about and then you somehow manage to become the perfectionist you are and do such a good job everyone wants to be you."

Brenna had to agree with her on the first part. "You're right, I am in a panic. I'm calling Alma to see what she thinks."

Callie grabbed Brenna's phone. "You will do no such thing. She's on her honeymoon. Not a good time for your theatrics."

Brenna frowned. "Theatrics? But Alma handles my meltdowns better than you do. She sometimes agrees with me."

"She talks you down so you can figure things out for yourself," Callie retorted, her fingers moving through an angel wing begonia. When she heard barking, she took off. "Great. Elvis is harassing my fish. Thanks."

Brenna wasn't through whining. She stared at a beautiful Japanese maple tree, wondering why her organization skills never made it to her love life.

"Wait," she said to the tree. "This is *not* my love life. This is my job. A temporary job that could lead to a bigger, better job." Instead of going into a panic about an interior designer named Serena, she should be thanking her lucky stars that she had this opportunity. Shaking her head, she whispered to the tree, "I hate it when my sister is right."

The tree sat still and regal, regarding her with a whisper of wind. Brenna stared through the branches toward the sky. *Lord, help me to stay focused and on target. And help me to remember what, not who, is the target.*

A butterfly fluttered by in shades of brown and gold.

Brenna tugged her notebook out of her tote and sketched the butterfly. Then she turned to see Callie laughing at Elvis as the big dog raced back and forth in front of the koi pond. The smile on her sister's face was so full of joy and contentment, Brenna had to capture it.

She quickly drew Callie's face and filled in her hair. She could see her sister sitting in a garden, wearing a pretty dress, with that smile on her face. Brenna wanted to paint that joy. She wanted Callie to find that joy again after overcoming breast cancer and a failed marriage.

She stopped, gasped and then grinned. "I think I've found myself again, *Mère*," she said to the sky. Her heart swelled with love and gratitude.

Callie came back down the aisle. "What are you up to now?"

Brenna grinned. "I'm all better now. I've got to get home. I want to do some research and I want to get out my brush sets and clean them."

Callie squealed so loud that Elvis woofed a bark in reply. "You're going to start painting again?"

"I think I am," Brenna said.

"What made you decide?"

She smiled at her sister. "Let's just say a butterfly fluttered by at exactly the right time."

Callie shrugged. "At least it got your mind off that Serena woman."

Brenna turned and waved. "Yes. Yes, it did."

For now, Brenna thought. Tomorrow might be different.

Brenna pulled up the long driveway to Fleur House on Tuesday morning and immediately noticed the sleek black luxury car that sat like a slinking panther next to Nick's work truck.

"Okay, so she looks *so* Houston," Brenna mumbled before she got out of her squat little economy car. "I look Baton Rouge, so I can deal."

Taking a breath, Brenna asked for strength and wisdom. *And dear Lord, don't let me bring out the drama.*

Walking up onto the limestone loggia at the entryway to the house, Brenna smoothed her denim pencil skirt and adjusted her plaid wool wrap. Brown, pointy-toed flat-heeled boots completed her work ensemble.

No drama. All business.

Following the sound of workmen talking and tools tinkling, Brenna marveled at the house all over again. This place would be a showpiece once it was completely renovated.

"Brenna, there you are."

She turned into the kitchen at the back of the long central hallway to find Nick standing next to a voluptuous older woman with rich black hair worn in a chignon. Dripping with gold jewelry, the woman looked as sophisticated as any art buyer Brenna had ever dealt with.

"Good morning," Brenna said, wondering who the visitor was. His mother maybe? Surely not Serena?

Nick stepped toward Brenna and tugged her into what would become the breakfast room. "Brenna, I want you to meet Serena. Serena Delrio, meet Brenna Blanchard."

"Lovely, *sí*," Serena said, smiling up at Nick while she took Brenna's hand and held it in hers. "Nicholas has told me so much about you, Brenna."

Brenna almost giggled in relief. "You're Serena?"

Serena looked confused, then a soft smile crested her wrinkle-free face. "*Sí*. I'm Nicholas's aunt. But sometimes he calls me *Abuela,* because I helped my younger sister raise the boy."

Brenna's gaze landed on Nick. He shrugged and smiled. "I told you you'd love her."

Brenna nodded. "It's nice to meet you, Ms. Delrio. Nick has told me a lot about you, too." But clearly, not enough.

Serena chuckled. "Call me Serena, please. I'm thinking he didn't tell you *everything* about me."

Nick grinned. "Where would be the fun in that, *Abuela?*"

Serena said something in rapid Spanish. "I think you let this poor girl believe I was a tyrant. Of course, I'm not." She crossed her arms. "However, I am a perfectionist."

Brenna breathed another sigh of relief. "Then I can assure you, we'll get along just fine."

Nick grinned at both of them. "I told you this would be interesting." He turned to Brenna. "My aunt has been decorating houses for close to thirty years."

"I started out as a gofer for a large firm in Houston and worked my way up. I went to design school on the company's dime. When the owner retired, I took over. He's still a silent partner, but I'm *la jefa.*"

"The boss," Nick explained.

"Got it," Brenna said, not so relieved now. Nick's aunt might not be young and tempting, but the woman was stylish, formidable and...intimidating. In an *abuela* kind of way.

Serena slapped her massive black leather satchel up onto the dusty counter. "Now, where do I find a good cup of coffee around here?"

Nick's eyes filled with panic, but Brenna took charge. "The coffee in Nick's trailer is more like swamp mud. But at my sister Alma's café in town, the coffee is rich and dark and good. I'd be glad to buy you a cup."

Serena's throaty laugh echoed out over the sound of hissing saws and heavy hammers. "Lead the way, *querida*."

"Hey, what about work?" Nick called.

"We are working," Serena answered. "You go on with your tearing down and rebuilding. We'll figure out the good stuff."

"That's what scares me," Nick said.

Brenna almost felt sorry for the man. Now he had two very opinionated women to deal with. And she had a feeling there *would* be drama. Lots of drama.

Chapter Eight

Brenna took Serena back behind the Fleur Café so she could see the Little Fleur Bayou and Alma's quaint cottage. Even though winter was coming, the walking trail along the bayou was still colorful and full of life. Palmetto palms swayed in the wind near the water's edge. Callie and her garden club friends had placed colorful pots of mums along the trail. She'd added pumpkins and hay bales here and there, giving the whole town a festive fall look. A chickadee frolicked in a red-leaf swamp maple while a snowy egret showed off underneath the vivid gold and rich red of a tallow tree.

"It's beautiful," Serena said. "Different from Houston and San Antonio." She held her coffee cup with both hands and breathed in the crisp air. "The cypress trees are lovely. I never knew they turned in the fall."

Brenna lifted her head. "The leaves are like old golden lace, or at least that's what my mother used to call them when they'd cushion the swamps. They completely disappear back into the earth. The winter trees stay draped in gray moss, but then in the spring, new leaves sprout out green."

"We must tell Callie to plant some cypress trees in the gardens at Fleur House, then," Serena said before taking a sip of her coffee. "And maybe more of those gorgeous maples, too."

"The old cypress trees that have been there for centuries are located down by the bayou," Brenna replied. "They're covered with Spanish moss. But I'm sure Callie will love to plant some fresh ones near the old fish pond and foundation in the back garden. And she loves swamp maples, too. She'll make sure the garden represents all of our plants and foliage."

"Good idea." Serena saw an old wooden bench underneath a moss-draped live oak. "Would you like to sit before we get back to work?"

Brenna nodded. "Yes. I've sure enjoyed talking to you about Fleur House. You already know as much about the house as I do."

Serena did her throaty laugh. "*Sí.* I love old estates. Such beauty. I cannot wait to get busy on decorating Fleur House. We'll have such fun together. We get the good job, traveling around for art and furnishings. I love my work."

Brenna liked Nick's aunt. "I have a confession to make," she said on a sheepish grin. "Nick didn't tell me you were his aunt. I imagined a young, attractive woman he'd probably dated or intended to date. Not that that mattered, except I felt threatened."

"I'm not young and attractive?" Serena quipped.

Brenna didn't know what to say until the older woman started laughing. "Nick has always had a mischievous side," she said. "I'm not so young and not so attractive, and I'm certainly not a threat. But why would you worry about such things?"

Brenna relaxed a little bit. "You are gorgeous and yes, attractive," she quickly clarified. "But you're also impressive. I can't wait to work with you." Then she shrugged. "I just came off a bad relationship, so my confidence, even in my career, is shaky."

"I see." Serena set down her empty coffee cup. "You worried that you'd be distracted by all the flirting and innuendos between Nick and this young, attractive woman?"

"That and what if she didn't like the art I wanted to place? What if she saw me as a threat to her and Nick? Silly things that aren't even important."

Serena's vivid dark eyes brightened. "Maybe not so silly. Have you already fallen for my nephew?"

That question threw Brenna. "No. I mean, he's hunky and intriguing, but I don't need a rebound relationship."

"Has he pursued you?"

"Pursued? No, we hardly know each other. And I made it clear that this would be a working relationship. So did he."

Very clear. So why was she telling his aunt all about it?

"Clear? Nick? That boy can't see the forest for the trees sometimes."

Brenna thought about that. "Actually, I haven't said that to him outright. I've mostly told myself that, in front of the mirror."

Serena cackled at that comment. "I'm not so worried about you, *querida*. But Nick, he hides his heart so well. He might try to persuade you, but then in the end, he'll be the one to bolt."

"I've already realized that," Brenna said. "And trust me, that's why I talk to myself in the mirror. I can't go back into that pattern of my falling for the worldly, successful man who keeps things too close to the chest. Besides, that only happens in books or movies. Not in real life." She shook her head. "I don't know why I even brought this up, except I want to assure you that I'm sticking to business."

"Pity," Serena said. She stood and touched a

hand to Brenna's shoulder. "Nick could use some-one like you in his life. He blames himself for things he had no control over."

Was Serena referring to his sister's death? Brenna almost asked what things, but she refused to pry about Nick behind his back. If the man wanted to tell her about his past, he'd do it in his own good time. She had to respect that he wasn't ready to talk about his issues, even if she'd vowed to never fall for another secretive man. Meantime, she had work to do. "Are you ready to go back to the house?"

Serena let out a contented sigh. "I suppose so. I'll be staying at Fleur Inn. I've already booked a room, but I can check in later. I travel light—just one big bag."

Brenna almost asked Serena to stay at her house, but that might be awkward with her papa coming and going at all hours.

"The inn is very comfortable and most of the rooms have a good view of both the big and the tiny bayou. If you need anything, let me know."

"I'll be fine," Serena replied. "But we might both get fired if we don't get back to the task at hand, *sí?*"

"So right on that," Brenna said. "Let's go get our stuff and get busy."

Together, they strolled back up to the café and entered through the back door.

Winnie was behind the counter, refilling the salad and pie cases. "Want dessert?"

Brenna glanced at Serena. "We could carry some back to the workers."

Serena chuckled. "The friendliest place on earth. And so generous!"

Winnie walked over to the glass-front cooler. "I have a fresh coconut pie and I just made a batch of oatmeal cookies."

"Both," Brenna replied. "I'll take some plates and plastic forks, too. And put it all on my tab. I'll be here later to work it off."

"Tell me you don't have two jobs?" Serena asked, her eyebrows quirking.

"Just until my sister Alma returns." She shrugged and looked sheepish. "I haven't really helped that much, not since Nick hired me, anyway."

"You do what you can, when you can." Winnie nodded. "Got it down on the order. And remind the construction crew that we can bring lunch out to them anytime if you call ahead and give us a count. Mollie and Pierre like to deliver on-site orders."

Mollie was a waitress here at the café and Pierre, who was Julien's younger brother, worked part-time here in the afternoons after he finished his welding job at the shipyard.

"They're saving up for their wedding in a year

or so," she explained after telling Serena about the young couple and their recent struggles.

"I'm sure Nick and his crew will order a lot of lunches," Serena replied.

"Good idea," Brenna said. "I can help deliver when Pierre's not around. A win-win situation."

Serena winked at Winnie. "In oh, so many ways."

"Tia Serena likes you," Nick told Brenna the next day.

Serena was in the house, measuring windows with some of the construction workers. Brenna and Nick were back in the trailer, going over some changes that had to be made in the staircase to accommodate a powder room in the central hallway. Nick wanted art pieces centered on each landing and there were three of them with wide staircases between each. But he also wanted to put a roomy downstairs powder room below the first landing. Brenna suggested a small table with a smaller painting over it near the door to the powder room. Nick seemed to agree on that idea.

"I like her, too," Brenna said. "We had a great lunch. Now that I've gotten to know her, I'm sure we'll work together just fine. She's a delight."

Nick gave her that look that held everything back while seeing everything she was trying to hide. "I never had any doubt. My aunt is one of the kindest, most faithful women I've ever known."

Shocked at his sincerity, Brenna ventured forth. "Do you have faith, Nick?"

He dropped the papers he'd been going over and stared out the tiny trailer window. "I have faith in things I can see and touch—like this house and my crew. I have faith in the people I care about, like my aunt and my parents. I have faith in you because I saw your passion the first time we talked about art."

Brenna couldn't stop herself. "And God? Do you have faith in God?"

He looked down, a frown darkening his face. "Is that important?"

"It is to me. I couldn't have gotten through my mother's illness and death without faith."

"And yet, it didn't save her. God didn't save her."

"No. He healed her in His own way, though."

"And this brings you comfort."

"Most days," she replied, wondering why she had even dared to bring this up.

He moved close, his face a dark mask of disdain. "And other days?"

"Other days, I miss my mama so much I ache with the pain and I hate the unfairness of it."

He stared at her for a long time, his eyes going ebony with an emotion that caused Brenna's heart to race. "Those days are the worst," he said on a whisper. Then he glanced at the old clock on the wall. "Time to go home."

Brenna glanced around. "I guess it is, for me, at least. I'll swing by the café and help Winnie for a couple of hours. That's part of my home."

"And me? I guess I should head home, huh?"

She saw the twist of humor on his face. "You're already home, right?"

Nick's smile was sharp and quick. "Yes, I am."

Brenna gathered her things and headed toward the door. Nick followed her, his hand automatically reaching out to guide her down the steps. "I'll see you tomorrow."

Brenna turned once she was on solid ground. "Oh, I just realized it's Wednesday night. Potluck at the church. You're always welcome to come. I think your aunt said she'd be there. She wants to meet everyone."

He rubbed a hand down his chin. "I have a lot of work."

"Of course." She turned to leave. But then she turned around to stare back up at him. "If you change your mind—"

"I won't."

With that, he shut the door and left her standing there in the gloaming.

Nick sat down to work, but his mind couldn't focus on the blueprints and construction reports on his desk. He needed to check on the permits and work on the purchase orders.

And yet, he couldn't get the scent of flowers out of his head. He inhaled and smelled the sweetness that Brenna had left behind. Getting up to head to the kitchen, Nick opened the small refrigerator and found a leftover piece of coconut pie.

He slammed the door and turned to lean against it. "Why does everyone around here love pie so much?"

And why did this tiny town always seem to congregate at the church?

He knew the answer to that one, of course. The church brought them comfort and companionship and...hope. Things he'd shunned for a long, long time now.

Brenna had no right to do this to him. No right to ask him about his faith. What did she know about his pain?

She lost her mother.

And you lost your sister.

She knows about pain.

"But not my pain," he said out loud.

Then he turned and pulled out the pie.

Dinner.

"I invited Nick to come, but he had work to do." Serena listened to Brenna while they walked through the receiving line. "I'm sure he did. My nephew is driven."

Brenna took that to mean "The boy is stubborn and tightly wound. He won't budge."

"Hey, Papa's here," Callie said as she hurried by Brenna. "I have to check on the lasagna."

"Need help?"

Callie shook her head. "No. You have a guest."

"I could help, too," Serena offered.

"Nonsense," Brenna said. "Callie is right. You're our guest."

"I enjoyed the devotional," Serena replied. "Your minister seems like a good man."

"The best," Brenna replied. "Reverend Guidry was right there with us when Mama got so sick. He stood by with us through her death and after. He's like a rock to us."

Serena glanced back over her shoulder. "You have a strong church family."

"Yes." Brenna didn't tell Serena that she'd all but abandoned that family when she moved to Baton Rouge. "It's good to be back in the fold."

Serena looked as if she wanted to say more, but hesitated.

"There's Daughter Number Three," Brenna's papa said behind her.

Brenna turned and grinned. "Are you trying to cut line, Papa?"

Her robust daddy chuckled and smiled over at Serena. "Maybe. I see we have a lovely guest tonight."

Serena actually batted her eyelashes. "*Sí.* I'm Serena Delrio, Nicholas Santiago's aunt."

"Is that a fact?" Papa's interested expression was almost comical. "Brenna, where are your manners? Aren't you gonna introduce us?"

"Uh, Papa, Serena just introduced herself. Serena, this is my papa, Ramon Blanchard."

Ramon extended his meaty hand to Serena. Instead of shaking her hand, however, he held it and almost bowed over it. "So nice to meet you. So glad to have you here tonight."

Serena's smile said it all. And so did Papa's antics.

Her daddy was flirting with Nick's aunt.

"Callie?" Brenna called, her hands suddenly sweaty. "I…I need to see you in the kitchen. Now."

Her sister put down the plate of French bread she'd carried to the buffet table and hurried into the kitchen.

"I'll be right back," Brenna told Serena and her daddy.

But neither was listening. Papa got in line behind Serena and explained the various Cajun dishes to her, and all with a smile on his face.

"What's the matter?" Callie said, her eyebrows shooting up.

"It's Papa," Brenna replied. "Look at him."

Callie took a covert glance out the pass-through window.

"He's in line, getting a meal."

"Look at him again and watch what he does each time he looks up at Nick's aunt."

Callie squinted and watched, then gasped. "Is our daddy flirting?"

"Yes," Brenna said. "He can't do that. He's not supposed to do that."

Callie looked again, then grinned big. "Says who?"

Brenna hit a palm on the old Formica counter. "Says me. I don't think it's right."

"Who are we to judge?" Callie asked, shrugging.

Brenna couldn't shrug this off. "I'm not judging. I'm just not comfortable with this."

Callie leaned close. "It's not about your happiness. If that woman makes our papa smile, then we need to leave them alone."

But Brenna couldn't do that. She wouldn't make a scene, but she'd sure have a talk with her daddy later.

And maybe Serena, too.

Callie must have sensed her intent. "Do not say anything, Bree. They're just talking."

"I won't embarrass you or them," Brenna said. "But I will talk to Papa later."

"Just be considerate," Callie said. "Please."

"I will."

She turned to go to the back of the line just as a few feet away a side door opened.

And in walked Nick Santiago.

Chapter Nine

Nick saw Brenna and walked toward her, all the while telling himself he only came to visit with his aunt.

Brenna's smile froze on her face. Was she mad because he'd turned her down earlier? Or was she upset that he'd shown up here, after all?

"Hola," he said, his discomfort making him itchy and nervous. "I'm a little late, but I'm hungry."

"You came to the right place, then," Brenna said. "We have lasagna, made with crawfish just for fun. And bread and salad and all kinds of side dishes."

"Can't wait." He saw his aunt with Brenna's daddy. "What's with those two?"

Brenna looked toward the round table where they'd settled with some other church members. "Well, they seem to have hit it off. My papa is a gentleman, so he probably felt obligated to make your aunt feel welcome."

"And my aunt is a lady, so she must have felt obligated to allow him that courtesy."

"Right."

Nick wasn't buying it. Brenna didn't look excited about her daddy sitting with his aunt. "You don't approve?"

"What's to approve? I'm not in charge of my daddy."

"But you think you should be?"

She shrugged and grabbed a big empty plate. "Somebody has to watch out for him."

Nick lifted his own plate. "And who looks out for you?"

"Me?" She grabbed a slab of buttered bread. "I've always been able to take care of myself."

Nick could believe that. She seemed capable. But did she have a clue that she was so obviously lonely and heartbroken?

"But you came home."

She turned, the lasagna spatula in her hand. "Yes, I came home because I was tired and burned-out and laid off and frustrated. Home is where I come when I need to get away from everything else."

Nick thought about that for a minute. "See, I'm the opposite. I move on to the next job and don't worry too much about getting away from everything."

"Really?" She slapped a big slab of steaming lasagna onto his plate. "So you'd rather run away from home than let someone see your weaknesses?"

He took his plate, winked at her then whispered in her ear, "I don't have any weaknesses."

He was rewarded with a huffy sigh behind him as he headed toward his smiling aunt.

Callie stared at Brenna so hard that Brenna fairly sizzled. "What?" she growled to her older sister.

"You're doing the drama-queen thing. Not very becoming."

"I am not. I'm tired and I ate too much lasagna."

"And two pieces of bread and four snickerdoodles."

Brenna glared back at her sister. "But who's counting?"

Callie ignored that and leaned close. "And already, you're mad at your new boss. That's been oh, almost two weeks of work, tops."

Brenna looked over at Nick. He raised his plastic cup of tea in a salute. "Great meal, ladies."

Papa nodded his agreement. "And great company, too." He smiled so big at Serena that Brenna wondered if his crowned teeth were going to burst.

"Thank you," Callie replied when Brenna didn't respond. "Mrs. LaBorde and her sewing circle had kitchen duty tonight. But I miss Alma's cooking. She ordered Winnie to take it easy while she's away because Winnie is running the café."

"Daughter Number Two—always thinking of others," Papa said, his hands on his rounded stomach. "Next week, our Alma will be back and then it will be gumbo night."

"And she's now a married woman," Brenna said, surprising the whole table. "Mrs. Julien LeBlanc."

"Did somebody mention my brother?" Pierre said from behind Brenna. He and his girlfriend, Mollie, better known as Pretty Mollie, were helping to clear the tables.

"We miss them," Callie replied, smiling at Mollie. "The café stays busy."

Mollie nodded. "But Winnie does a great job of keeping us all on our toes. She doesn't mess around."

"You young folk need that kind of authority," Papa said, but his smile was indulgent. "Have you met Nick's aunt Serena?"

"I met her at the café," Mollie said, waving across the table at Serena. "Pierre, this is Miss Serena, Nick's aunt. I told you about Nick, remember?"

Pierre reached out to shake Nick's hand. "I

talked to him the other day. I might help do some of the welding around the house, if he needs me."

Nick gave Brenna a quick glance, then nodded. "I can always use experienced welders. I also hired some of those buddies you brought by the other day when I had the open call for jobs. I appreciate it."

"So do they," Mollie replied, slapping Pierre on the arm.

Papa grinned up at them. "I'm proud of you, Pierre. And I'm sure your *maman* is, too."

Pierre squirmed and tried to look sullen, but it didn't work. "She's waving at me now. Guess I'd better go see what she wants."

Nick laughed as they gathered dishes and hurried away. "I remember that age." He looked down at his plate.

Serena leaned back in her chair. "So do I. Thought your poor mama was going to have a breakdown."

"I did give her and daddy cause for a lot of worry," Nick replied. "I'm surprised they're still speaking to me."

The table went quiet while Brenna wondered with a burn that surpassed the tangy crawfish lasagna what had shaped Nick into the man he'd become. He was obviously successful and well-respected. His work crew hung on his every word and worked hard. But he also had a brooding quality that probably scared people away. Especially women.

Maybe her, she told herself. Or she'd be wise to realize that. She wondered about his sister and what had happened. Maybe Serena would tell her the truth, but she'd rather hear it from Nick.

Before she knew it, everyone had left the table and she was sitting there staring across at Nick.

"What are you thinking?" he asked. He got up to come around and sit next to her.

Brenna blinked, wondering what to say to him. "I was concerned earlier about Papa and your aunt. But I think I've decided I like the idea of their being friends. Papa hasn't smiled like that in a very long time."

"You can handle that, really?" His dark eyes told her he didn't believe her.

"I can. I know I'm bossy and interfering, but I also want my papa to be happy. I'd be selfish to stand in the way of that."

He laughed, then chewed on a chunk of crushed ice. "Relax. They've only just met. I think it will all work out."

Maybe that was a hint for her to back off on him, too.

"You think so?"

He touched a finger to her hair, then dropped his hand back onto his lap. "I think everything will work out for the best."

Brenna had to know. "Why did you decide to come to dinner?"

He shook his head. "I ate the last of the coconut pie but I needed more." His gaze swept over her face. "I was still hungry."

Brenna's pulse went up a notch, the beating against her temple merging with the shivers of heat moving through her system. "And now?"

He got up. "Let's go outside."

She glanced around, saw Callie giving her a questioning look. Her sister nodded and pointed to the doors. "Go," Callie mouthed.

"What about your aunt?"

"She knows her way back to the inn across the street."

"Or Papa will make sure she gets home."

"Right."

They went out the same side door he'd entered earlier.

Once they were alone underneath an ancient magnolia tree, she asked, "What's the matter, Nick? Can't breathe in there?"

He laughed. "I just needed some air."

Brenna pushed at her hair and adjusted her wrap. "It was a bit stifling inside. We had a big crowd tonight."

He looked back at the glowing lights on the church porch. "It's a welcoming place and I'm sorry about earlier. I didn't mean to disrespect your church or your faith."

"I understand." She waited, hoping he'd open up.

"Wanna walk for a while?"

Brenna knew she wasn't going to get much more out of the man. And what did it matter? He would only be here for a short time. Once the house was done, he'd pack up that trailer and drive away, off to another challenge.

And he'd forget all about her.

They walked along the piers and docks surrounding the Big Fleur Bayou that was part of the Intracoastal Waterway. Brenna had grown up walking these trails and boardwalks. But tonight, with Nick beside her, everything looked new and mysterious.

Because she was with a new and mysterious man.

"We have to work together," Nick said, taking her hand in his. "I tell myself that, but—"

"You already regret hiring me?"

"No, not at all. You've been a big help these last few days. And you're a lot better looking than most of the construction crew. But I need you to understand…I don't normally react to women the way I've reacted to you."

Brenna's heart did a little bouncing flip. "Is that a good or bad reaction?"

He stopped underneath a tall palm tree and turned to stare down at her. "Both."

Brenna knew this was a defining moment in their fledging relationship. She decided to let him off the hook. "I don't expect anything from you, Nick. We have a working relationship. Nothing more."

"No, nothing more," he said. "It's better that way, I think." His tone sounded final while his eyes told her he wanted something more.

Brenna waited, wondering what she should do next. Turn and run. Stay and fight. Accept? Be professional and shake his hand? Forget work and go for the romance?

No. She knew how that would end. She needed this job more than she needed another brooding, hard-to-understand man in her life.

Nick lifted his hand, his fingers trailing through her bangs. "You should wear your hair down more often."

She smiled to hide the warmth shivering down her spine. "Is that a work requirement?"

"No, that's a Nick requirement. But then, that's part of the problem. I shouldn't be making such requests. It's distracting."

"To me or you?"

He repeated a word he'd used earlier. "Both."

Brenna had to smile at that. "I don't want to distract you. I want to make this restoration the best possible."

"So do I," he said. He held his hand in her hair.

Brenna felt the warmth and strength of his touch through her skin, through her heart. "Then we shouldn't worry about the rest, right?"

"Right." He pulled her close. "I just need to clear up one thing."

Brenna didn't know how to read this man. His eyes were shimmering and inky like the bayou waters. His smile was secretive and compelling, like the vast swamps that stretched to the Gulf. His touch was like the wind, both cool and warm at the same time.

"Nick?"

He leaned down and kissed her, the touch of his mouth on hers drawing her, molding her, branding her. He tasted like the mint tea from Alma's café. He stopped, his lips grazing hers, waiting, testing.

Brenna's mouth touched his and held tight. He responded by taking her into his arms. For a few precious seconds, she was out in that vast water, floating underneath a crescent moon, her life complete and at peace.

He pulled back to stare down at her, his eyes black with a new awareness. "Well, that didn't work."

"What was that?" she asked between quick breaths.

"That was me, trying to get you out of my head."

"And it didn't work?"

"Not so much."

"What do we do now?"

Brenna knew what she wanted to do. She wanted to kiss him again, but he wanted a working relationship, not a love affair.

"We keep on at it. We get the job done. That's all we can do." He touched his hand to her face. "That's all I can offer, Brenna."

She pulled away. "Relax. I wasn't expecting anything more."

He stared down at her and then dropped his hand away. "I shouldn't have kissed you."

Anger colored the night and hid her embarrassment and disappointment. "Then why did you?"

"I thought this…feeling…would burn itself out if I did."

"But that didn't work for you?"

"No." He turned and leaned over the iron railing and stared down into the water. "It only made this worse."

She understood what the man was trying to say. "*This* being you and me, kissing, being aware of each other. This won't help your goal—to restore this house and move on, right?'

He pivoted toward her. "Right. I have to do my job and I have obligations. I need you to understand."

"What I understand is that you just kissed me

and now you're regretting that to the point that I'm insulted."

He looked shocked, then sheepish. "I didn't intend to insult you. I…I enjoyed kissing you. A lot."

"But you can't do it again because it will interfere with your carefully controlled plan, which is to do your job and then hook up your little trailer and get on down the road."

"Yes," he said, trying to reach for her again. "You mess with my head, Brenna. You mess with all of my carefully controlled plans. I'm not sure how to handle you."

Brenna had enough. She hadn't exactly thrown herself at him. "I get it, Nick. But like you said, we need to relax. This will all work itself out. You don't need to worry. I'm a big girl. I know the rules. And I don't spend every waking breath pining away for you. I don't really know you and I'm pretty sure that's the way you want to keep it. Because you don't want me to know you. You don't want the Lord to know you. That's why you didn't want to come to church. You felt exposed and vulnerable and afraid. And now, to make things worse, you kissed me when you really didn't want to. I understand."

"You don't understand," he said, anger making his accent more pronounced. "You will never understand."

"Probably not, but that doesn't mean I can't

mind my own business and do my job. No more kissing the boss for me."

She pivoted to head back to her car. The wind had turned cold, but the shivers crawling down her back weren't coming from the cold air. This coldness poured over her heart with a solid, freezing pain. Nick Santiago didn't know how to love anyone else. Because he couldn't love himself.

Brenna heard footsteps behind her, heard him call her name. But she wasn't going to turn back. She wouldn't let this man break her heart so soon after Jeffrey had hurt her so badly.

"Help me, Lord," she whispered to the night. She still had a lot of spiritual growing to do. But falling back into a destructive pattern wouldn't help that growth.

Nick was a temptation. A temptation she had to avoid.

But the test would be working with him every day while she tried to overcome that way he made her feel.

"Brenna?" he called behind her. "Are you all right?"

She turned at her car. "I'm fine, Nick. I'll be okay. I think you need to ask yourself that question, though." She pulled her keys out and unlocked the door. "Tell your aunt good-night for me. I'll see you tomorrow."

She got in and sped away before he could answer. But his lonely shadow stood in the night, silhouetted by a bayou moon. She couldn't get that image out of her head.

Chapter Ten

The last week of October went by in a blur for Brenna. She hadn't been out to Fleur House much this week because she had a copy of the layout and she and Serena had gone over the color schemes for the main downstairs rooms and all of the bedrooms and baths. Serena would coordinate the decor of each room with Brenna, so that together they could create rooms that pleased both Nick and the new owner. Most of that could be done online and with lots of phone conversations for now.

She could shop and bid for art pieces online and have them ordered and ready when the rooms were completely finished. Because she had so many contacts, she'd already planned a trip to New Orleans and a weekend back in Baton Rouge to shop for interesting items and pieces. Callie and Alma had jumped on the New Orleans trip, wanting to make it a sister act. That was fine with Brenna as long as they let her do her job. When she'd asked Serena to go with her to Baton Rouge, Nick's aunt had clapped her hands together in glee.

"We can combine Christmas shopping with work. A perfect trip."

Brenna had to admit she really loved Nick's Tia Serena. Serena was a combination of Earth Mother and a flamboyant, eclectic "crazy aunt." Everyone should have somebody like Serena in their family, Brenna decided. Whether Nick called her *Tia* or *Abuela,* Brenna could tell how close they were.

Her papa might agree with that because he and Serena had spent a lot of time together over the past few days.

Now if she could only get along so well with the nephew. While their working relationship was polite and above reproach, something had shifted after Nick had tried to kiss her out of his mind.

She couldn't get him out of her mind.

And from the way she'd spot him staring at her, Brenna was pretty sure he hadn't managed to put her out of his thoughts, either. But they were both too stubborn to explore that little problem. So they worked—sometimes apart, sometimes together.

She'd hated to see Serena leave yesterday.

Serena had not divulged what had happened to Nick's sister, but she had given Brenna a parting warning about that one. "He's a brooder. He hurts, but hides his pain behind his work. He's driven, Brenna. Driven by regret and an unforgiving mind-set. He needs the love of Christ back in his heart. We can't put it there for him. He has to find it on his own. But we can certainly pray for him."

And so that's what Brenna was trying to do. Pray for Nick every day, while she prayed for her family and her own scorched heart. "I don't know, Lord. This is new and different and I don't remember praying this much for Jeffrey."

Maybe she should have. Or maybe Nick was different from Jeffrey, after all. Remembering how her mother had comforted her once after a high school breakup, Brenna thought about her mother's reassuring words.

"God puts people in our paths for a reason, belle. It's not your time to fall in love. You're young still. When the time is right, you'll know because it will be in God's plan for you."

Maybe, maybe. Or maybe she was reading all the signs wrong.

So here she sat on a Friday afternoon, out on the screened porch of her papa's house, her home, her safe place. Shuffling through her files, Brenna shut down her laptop and stared out at the beginnings of a brilliant sunset over the water. Fleur was known for throwing festivals in spring, summer, fall and winter. Tonight was the Harvest Festival at the church. It would spill out onto the main street through town, the street that followed the big bayou. Vendors would put out their wares and Alma, bless her heart, would cook up some of her famous gumbo. Brenna expected even more crowds of tourists for that because Alma had partnered with the famous chef and newspaper columnist Jacob Sonnier to mass-produce her gumbo to supermarkets across the South.

"Another hot night on the bayou in good ol' Fleur," Brenna said into the wind. Out on the water, a crappie jumped and splashed while blue jays chirped and fussed in the nearby swamp maple. "I need to go get some of that gumbo," she told the noisy little birds. "Pronto."

And she wouldn't worry about Nick and his Friday-night plans. She could picture him in that drab trailer, poring over blueprints and permits, his laptop buzzing with a glow of churning battery power, his fingers moving in a dance across the keyboard. He might look up and out at the big house that was slowly changing into a fine estate. He might even wonder what it would be like to have such a home or any home at all.

And he might even think of her.

Maybe, just maybe.

Brenna finished her work, then got up to change for the festival. She didn't intend to sit around pining away on such a lovely night. She needed people and laughter and some good zydeco. That's what she needed.

He needed to get some air.

Nick looked up and realized the sun was setting out beyond the open door of his trailer. Everyone else had left long ago and now the quiet was mocking him, taunting him with a humming buzz that sounded like cicadas. He got up to stare across at the house. The facade had changed from a muted grayish-white stone to a bright, gleaming fresh white that shimmered in the golden sunset. Even with scaffolding all around it, the house seemed to be happy and proud, ready to begin a new life with new memories.

That, he loved about his job. He liked to leave a place better than he'd found it. It was one of the biblical principles his parents had taught him.

Nick ran a hand down his neck. He hadn't thought about the Bible in a long time. He needed to call his mother. Maybe he needed to do a quick run to San Antonio for a visit.

But tonight, he felt restless and alone. Tonight, he needed…something. Remembering the big sign he'd seen earlier in town, he thought about the Harvest Festival going on at the church.

Did he want to get in the thick of things?

Or did he just want to be near Brenna?

Without thinking about it too much, he hurried

to get a quick shower and a change of clothes. He'd heard a lot about Alma LeBlanc's gumbo. High time he tried it out for himself.

Brenna watched Alma dancing with Julien. They seemed so happy. Ashamed that she's had a flash of jealousy at her sister's wedding, Brenna lifted up a prayer of thanks that Alma was happily married and so far, safe from breast cancer. Callie hadn't been so lucky, but even after her divorce, she'd survived for five years now. Brenna had a mammogram every year like clockwork. They'd all promised their mother they'd do that for her. But the thought of inheriting the dreaded disease was always with them.

Watching Alma now, Brenna smiled and remembered how hard Julien had fought to win back Alma's heart. Brenna could only dream of having a man fight for her like that. Jeffrey certainly hadn't. She turned to go back inside the church to check on more baked goods to sell at the dessert booth.

Turned and saw a tall man wearing a leather jacket with jeans and cowboy boots walking through the crowd.

Nick Santiago.

Why did her heart lift and dance along with the feisty zydeco? Other than the necessary meetings, she'd tried to avoid him this week. They'd been polite and to the point regarding what was expected of her, but each time she'd been around the man, she'd felt an undercurrent between them that raged worse than the Mississippi River. Brenna didn't want to be taken under by that strong pull, but how could she avoid it?

Nick looked up and right into her eyes.

No way out now.

"Hello," she said, waiting as he walked toward her.

"Hi." His gaze swept over her, taking in her wool jacket and jeans over her flat-heeled boots. "Nice night. How's the festival going?"

"Big crowd," she said, hoping her anticipation and apprehension didn't show on her face. "I think the church will make a lot of money for the next mission trip to Grande Isle."

"What do they do down at Grand Isle?"

"Rebuild," she replied. "Always rebuild. Hurricanes love that little barrier island."

He put his hands in the pockets of his jeans. "I've never been there."

"Well, sign up for the trip. They're going in about two weeks."

He nodded. "Depends on how the house is going."

She doubted he'd go on any mission trip. Why should he? He had an air-tight alibi—he worked day and night. She might go on the trip because her hours were pretty much her own. "I've been a couple of times. It's a wonderful place. Not resort territory, but wild and beautiful all the same."

He stared at her, the words *wild and beautiful* echoing between them. He changed the subject to avoid the obvious. "I came for some gumbo."

"Oh, well, then let me take you to the gumbo booth over in the café parking lot. I haven't had any yet and I'm hungry, too."

He lifted his chin. "Then we can eat together."

She laughed. "Have you noticed everything revolves around food in our town?"

"Yep, but I kind of like that. A good meal always brings people together."

"It's never stopped my family from coming together that's for sure. When my mama was alive, we used to celebrate every holiday with a big meal. We'd invite lots of people because she always cooked too much food. Always."

"That sounds nice."

"It was. My papa can cook, too. It's great, but it's not the same."

He stopped her before they crossed the closed-off street. "Brenna, I'm sorry I've been so distant this week. I didn't mean to let this happen."

Bracing herself, Brenna asked, "What's happened, other than we decided we'd stick to a strictly professional relationship?"

He didn't answer at first. "Nothing's happened,

but I don't feel as close to you as I did when I first hired you. I enjoyed our friendship. Do we still have a friendship?"

She didn't want to complicate things, but he'd set the stipulations so he had to deal with them. "We don't have to be best buddies, Nick. We have a job to do and that's what we're focusing on right now." At the look of defeat in his eyes, she added, "But we can be friends. I'd like that. I don't usually work very well with someone who resents me."

"I don't resent you," he said, guiding her through the foot traffic. "I don't know what I feel."

Brenna didn't know what she felt, either. Except that each time she was around him, Nick made her get all gooey and soft-centered. He melted away that hard core she'd place around her heart after she and Jeffrey had parted ways. But it was too soon to tell if she was grasping at a relationship or if this could be something more. Was Nick the one her mother had promised would come?

"Look," she said before they went to order their gumbo, "we can agree that we're attracted to each other. Is that so difficult to admit?"

He shook his head. "No. I mean, I think that was clear last week after we…kissed each other."

She closed her eyes to that particular memory. "Okay. So we have to work together for a few months, at least. But what's to hold us apart after that?"

He stared down at her with those dark, probing eyes. "I don't know about that, either."

"Because you'll move on?"

"Yes. I always move on."

She had already figured that one out, so she shouldn't have even suggested anything else. "Then I guess we'll just chalk this up to bad timing and your definite lack of commitment."

He tugged her by her elbow. "Whoa. My lack of commitment? I thought you were just as confused as I am."

"Oh, I'm confused all right. But I'm willing to explore the possibilities even though I've been through a rough time in the love department. Nick, I'm not ready to rush into anything, but I don't mind getting to know you."

"But you don't *see* me getting to know you? You don't think I can relax in the moment?"

"No, I think you're afraid to hint at anything more because you're so afraid I might jump on you like a duck on a june bug."

He actually smiled at that. "A duck on a june bug? How does that work exactly?"

She started walking again. "You know what I mean. The duck eats the little bug. Then there's nothing left. I'm not quite that bad."

He caught up with her. "You're right. You're not

quite that bad. You're more like a ladybug, flying in and settling down. If I remember correctly, ladybugs bring good luck."

"Not in this case," she said over her shoulder.

Stopping her again, he said, "Can we just start over? Maybe take things a little slow? I've never been good at rushing a project."

"Is that what I am to you, Nick? A project?"

"No, I didn't mean it that way. I...I need you to understand...this is new to me."

"And I'm an old pro at bad relationships?"

"No. I don't want to hurt you." He looked out over the crowd, then glanced back at her. "But I don't want to be hurt, either."

Brenna took in a breath. "Well, at least admitting that is the first step. We can agree on that, too."

He nodded, his expression relaxing. "Can we eat now? I'm starving."

"C'mon, cowboy. You'll feel better after some gumbo and corn bread. Everyone always does."

He grinned for the first time tonight. "That sounds good. Really good."

"So good, it'll make you want to slap your mama," she quipped. "In a good way, I mean."

He followed her to the big booth, then leaned close to whisper in her ear. "I'm glad we had this discussion. I think we've reached a new compromise. In a good way, I mean."

"We'll see," she said, her mind whirling with confusion and hope. Compromise, if she considered that he'd once again warned her away with excuses and man-type reasoning. Did it really matter? He'd be gone soon and she'd have to decide where she wanted to go from here. "Only time will tell."

But they didn't have a whole lot of time.

She sure intended to make the best of the time they did have, however. Brenna had fought against her curious nature to preserve her job status. But that might change now. She'd do a good job, she had no doubt about that. But if Nick had feelings for her, she'd also push to bring those feeling to the surface.

Because she couldn't let him walk away without exploring the feelings they had for each other. Giving up had never been her thing. Brenna would fight to the finish to get to the truth.

But that might mean going into Nick's past to figure out why he was so afraid of loving again.

Chapter Eleven

The next morning, Brenna was back on the porch with Alma and Callie. They'd agreed to have an early breakfast with their dad before they all went their separate ways on what looked to be a busy Saturday.

"Okay," Alma said, her quiet tone always soothing. "You've told us all about Fleur House and all about Aunt Serena. We want to hear more about Nick now."

Brenna played with her napkin. "But aren't you concerned about Papa getting so close to another woman?"

Callie made a face, then glanced at Alma. Pointing at Brenna, she said, "*She's* not so keen on Papa being with another woman is what she meant to say."

Brenna bristled. "Well, doesn't it bother y'all? Besides, I am trying to tolerate Papa and Serena together."

Alma put her hands under her chin and leaned on the table. "I have to admit, it seems strange. But it's been over five years since Mama died. He hasn't looked at another woman even though he's always polite and nice to the church widows who've tried to get his attention."

"So maybe he's just being nice to Serena," Callie offered. She nabbed another strawberry and nibbled on it. "She was visiting and he knows she'll be working with you, Bree."

Brenna took a sip of her coffee. "No, it's more than just being nice. I've seen his nice persona. This went beyond that. He saw Serena standing there at church the other night and, well, something changed in him. He had that look that he used to get when Mama would walk into a room." She shrugged. "I think that's what got to me."

"Are you sure it was 'the look'?" Alma asked, tossing her dark curls off her shoulder. "I mean there's a look and then there's 'the look.'"

Brenna thought about the way Julien looked at Alma, the way her daddy had looked at her mama. And the way Nick had looked at her once or twice. "It was a look—maybe not the same one he gave Mama, but still…he was interested. And Serena is an attractive woman."

"With Latin blood," Callie added. "I think they make a good match."

"You're a hopeless romantic, too," Alma retorted. "Bree, has Papa said anything to you about Serena?"

"Not really. We don't mention it. I've avoided the discussion because I didn't want to do what I usually do—make a mountain out of a molehill—as Mama used to say."

"Well, that's wise," Alma said. "Considering you have to work with both Nick and his aunt, if you got all upset about this, it could make things awkward for everyone."

"Not any more awkward than Nick kissing me and then telling me he regretted it."

Alma squealed. "Now we're getting somewhere. I have to hear more about this."

"Did you overreact to that?" Callie asked, her eyes burning with questions.

Brenna rubbed a finger down her coffee mug. "I tried not to, but it was hard. I'm working on getting better in the overreacting department. I really like Serena, though. I'm just trying to imagine Papa with someone else."

Alma looked from Callie to Brenna. "She's not going to tell us about Nick or that kiss until we settle this." She took Brenna's hand. "Listen, it'll be hard to see Papa with someone else, but I'd rather have him with someone and happy than alone and lonely. I mean, really happy. So we have to decide if we can handle this or…break his heart all over again."

"I vote we handle it," Callie said, raising her hand. "And I really need to get to the garden center, so you need to tell us more about Nick, and right now. I left Elvis with one of the workers and that dog knows how to sweet-bark all of 'em."

Alma got up, too. "I agree. I have to go, too. Let's get to Nick."

"What about him?" Brenna asked, already knowing the answer. "He's not ready for a relationship— end of discussion."

Alma started clearing away their dishes. "Oh, I don't know about that. I want to hear about how he met you at my wedding and you danced together and then he hired you right away. About how you two seem to sizzle like crawfish hitting boiling water whenever you're together. Let me see, did I forget anything, Callie?"

Brenna let out a groan. "Crawfish? Seriously? I can't believe you two. It's not like that."

Callie laughed while she gathered muffins and fruit to take back into the house. "Oh, yes, it is so that way. But you don't see it. Kinda like Alma and Julien and their ten years of ignoring each other on purpose. Yeah, right."

Alma grinned and looked all dreamy. "Yeah, right."

Brenna's gaze followed her prissy older sister. "I hope one day we get to pick on her and dissect her love life."

"Her turn will come," Alma said on a smile. "But, Bree, are you interested in Nick Santiago?"

"He's an interesting man," Brenna quipped. "Hard to miss."

"But are you really interested?"

Brenna opened the door so Alma could bring in the coffeepot. "I might be. But the subject in question has made it clear he does not feel the same. Our kiss was the best. We connected."

"If you locked lips, I'd say you sure did," Callie retorted with a grin. "Winnie said he called you *fascinating.*"

That surprised Brenna. "Really? Maybe that's why he decided to kiss me—to see if I'm as fascinating as I seem."

Alma grinned at Callie. "Well, that's a start."

"But he got all upset about it and apologized and backpedaled around things. The man can't wait to get this job finished so he can move on to the next one."

"Really? That's a shame." Alma rinsed out the coffee decanter and made sure the coffeemaker was off. "He seems so intense. And so interested in you."

"Good word for it—*intense,*" Brenna replied. "Too intense. He's a bit commitment—shy, I think."

"Why is that?" Callie asked.

Brenna knew she could trust her sisters. "Something about his sister. She died when they were young. That's all I know, but I think it must have something to do with that."

"Oh, how tragic," Alma replied. "Maybe he's never gotten over losing her and so he's afraid to love again. Same as Papa. Love, even love between siblings, can do strange things when you throw grief into the mix."

"Or guilt," Callie added. "Maybe he feels somehow responsible?"

"I never thought of that," Brenna replied, her mind whirling. "And the one time we talked about it, he said it was complicated and he didn't want to discuss it." She shrugged. "And for once in my life, I didn't push the issue. I wanted to keep my job and honestly, I wanted to keep my friendship with Nick. But that was before he kissed me and made me see that he feels more than friendship. And that he's fighting how he feels."

"You might need to gently ask about the sister," Alma suggested. "At the right time, of course."

Callie stood by the stove, staring at them. "He's never mentioned a sister to me. He's close to his parents, but I only found that out when he came in to order flowers for his mother's birthday. I mean, he seemed close to them. But he did say he hasn't been very good about going home for visits."

"They are close," Brenna said. "But something happened back then and he's made it clear he doesn't want to talk about it or deal with it. He never goes home because he is a workaholic. He prefers work to getting into issues."

"I can do an online search," Callie suggested.

"No." Brenna glared at her sister. "I want him to trust me enough to tell me himself, so back off." Then she stared down at the floor. "Besides, I already vetted him when I agreed to work for him. The only thing I found was a picture—a painted portrait of a girl named Jessica. I'm pretty sure the portrait was of his little sister. I got interrupted and never went back to read the article. It seemed…intrusive."

"Our nosy little sister is growing up," Alma said with a smile. "But now we all want to know what's in that article, of course."

"No," Brenna said. "You both have to promise me you won't snoop. I really want him to trust me enough to tell me himself. I used to snoop on Jeffrey and that only brought heartache. I saw pictures of him online, remember? Him with other women, laughing and posing. He didn't even care if I saw them. He always brushed it off as friends having fun."

"Well, this is different," Alma said. "If he feels responsible for his sister's death, this could explain Nick's so-called issues."

"I said, leave it alone," Brenna replied. "I mean it."

Callie held up her hands. "Okay. My lips are zipped."

Alma nodded. "Mine, too. I promise."

"Thank you," Brenna said. "He'd never trust me if he finds out we've been snooping behind his back. He'd never trust any of us again."

"She's right." Alma started gathering her stuff. "Callie has a stake in this, too, because she'll be working on the gardens next spring. Me, I don't have time to spy. I have more gumbo to get out and a café to run. I've abused Winnie enough, making her do both her work and mine."

"She loves it," Brenna said. She waved bye to her sisters and turned to finish up the dishes. Papa had headed out right after breakfast to take a group of tourists on a swamp tour, which left her with the whole morning open.

She thought about doing some more online research. She wanted to find the perfect centerpiece to put on the heavy tiger oak table Serena had found for the entryway.

But when she pulled up Google, her mind wondered to Callie's earlier suggestion regarding Nick's sister. That picture and article might explain a whole lot. If the Jessica she'd glimpsed was even Nick's sister. It could be another Jessica Santiago. She ought to check to be sure.

"I can't do that," Brenna told herself. "I can't."

But why couldn't she? If she found something and never mentioned it to Nick, what would be the harm?

The harm would be in her withholding what she'd found. She couldn't do that to Nick. Maybe he'd talk about his sister in God's own time. Or maybe her death had nothing to do with his attitude now.

On the other hand, maybe Brenna would understand him a little better if she had some idea of what had happened. Besides, there might not be any information online. Did she dare check to see?

"No." She got up and headed upstairs. Instead of work, she decided she'd paint. So she took the sketch of Callie and played with it a bit. Maybe she'd drive out to Fleur House tomorrow afternoon and take advantage of the wonderful light in the sunroom. Callie against the gardens of Fleur House—that would make a nice gift for her sister's upcoming birthday. She'd paint Callie from the sketch and add in the flowers and garden later.

And that would be time well spent. Much better than trying to figure out Nick Santiago by doing an internet recon search.

She didn't want to do a search on Nick. She wanted Nick to feel comfortable enough around her to tell her everything about himself. After all, that kind of intimacy was what made a love affair special and timeless.

"When are you coming home for a visit?"

Nick held the phone away and smiled. It was a beautiful Sunday afternoon and he'd felt restless. So he'd called home, dreading this conversation, but enduring it each time he talked to his mother. "Soon, *Madre,* soon. I have a lot of work to do before I can leave the crew here alone." He used the same old excuses each time they talked, but his mother wouldn't give up.

"Nicky, you work too hard," his mother replied. "Serena told me how when she was there you didn't stop to eat, barely to sleep. Why do you insist on doing this to yourself?"

They'd been down this road before. If his mother had her way, Nick would stay in his little hacienda and eat all of his meals at home with his parents. Oh, and marry a nice girl from the local community, preferable handpicked by her. She wanted to make him happy, but they both knew only he could do that.

His parents worried about him, prayed for him, hoped for him. But they couldn't fix the part of him that was shattered and broken. And they pretended that they weren't the same.

But his whole family was still in a deep state of grief. And a deep state of denial.

"I like my work," he said, pushing away the dark memories. "I'm okay. I stay in shape because I'm always moving and climbing. I eat good food here. The best."

"Better than my tamales?"

"Not that good," he replied, laughing. "I hope to be home soon, I promise. Tomorrow, I have to do a walk-through with the roofers and later this week I have a plumber coming back to finish up with the piping for the bathrooms."

"Your mind, it's always spinning."

"Yes, it is," Nick agreed. "I promise to call more often and to come visit soon."

"Serena also told me about this woman—Brenna. Serena thinks you two would make a perfect match."

Nick had expected this. "Serena only saw us working together for the most part. Brenna is a nice woman, but she's not interested in me." Or, at least, he'd pushed Brenna away from being interested in him. He was having a much harder time following the same advice.

Jeanette Santiago let loose in rapid Spanish. Settle down, find a nice girl, make me some grandbabies before I become an old woman. "I think that's the other way around. You need to find a good woman, Nicky. Bring her and let me meet her. I will know in my heart if she is the one for you."

"Isn't it better if *I* know in *my* heart, Mama?"

"Your heart is too bruised and battered to see what could be something good in your life."

He'd certainly heard it all before. At least this time she'd left out the lecture about letting go of the past and things he couldn't change.

Only this time, Nick actually took his mother's words under consideration. Brenna was something good in his life. And if he messed things up with her, she'd go running in the other direction. Did he want that? Or did he want to finally admit he'd like to have some of those dreams his mother dreamed for him? He roamed around the big, empty house, checking walls, noticing new fixtures. His eyes landed on the mural Brenna loved so much. The mural he'd saved for her.

"I'll consider bringing her to meet you," he finally said. "That might be a good idea, just to see…"

"Serena was right, then. You do have feelings for this girl."

Nick didn't argue with his mother because he knew the truth. This woman was different. This time, he'd felt a little tug in his heart that had broken through some of his guilt and pain. But would a tug lead to something else? Nick still wasn't sure how to handle this, but he couldn't keep denying that he had feelings for Brenna. These past few weeks, being around her, getting to know her, had changed him.

After hanging up, he gathered some papers and decided he'd ride into town and find a nice booth at the back of Fleur Café. Maybe he could get some of this necessary paperwork out of the way if he got out of this trailer and away from the big house. A few weeks until Thanksgiving and things were a little behind, but they could make it up if they had good weather. And if he could keep his mind off Brenna Blanchard.

"At least we're just about done with hurricane season," he mumbled as he got in his car and headed into town.

Chapter Twelve

She'd again been at Fleur House all afternoon. Brenna had made sure Nick wasn't around before she'd unlocked the big house and went inside. This was the second Sunday she'd enjoyed the quiet sanctuary of the house while she painted. Alma's weekend crew had let it slip that Nick liked to come to the café on Sunday afternoons to work quietly and drink gallons of coffee.

"And he eats pie," Alma had confided. "He seems to like pie."

No one other than Alma knew she'd been coming here. Not even Nick. She really wanted to surprise Callie with this portrait. But she also wanted to do this one thing simply because it brought her joy and made her feel closer to God.

It had been such a long time since Brenna had taken things slow and easy and actually enjoyed the beauty of a Sunday afternoon after church and dinner with her family. This time helped her to relax and reflect and see that she'd been living a spiraling, stressed life in Baton Rouge. Being back home had seemed like the worst thing at first, but being here now and being a part of this important restoration had helped her to see that she needed to do her own restoration, too.

Today, however, the sun wasn't shining through the ceiling-to-floor arched windows. The weatherman had predicted rain beginning tomorrow and lasting all week. The outer bands of the tropical disturbance were stirring around out in the Gulf. Brenna finished up and gathered her brushes, easel and other supplies, glad that she'd had a couple of hours to touch up the portrait. She'd talked to Callie so much about which plants and flowers she favored that Brenna knew them by heart. No sunflowers, but Callie loved old magnolias and crape myrtles, moss-covered cypress trees and trailing bougainvilleas. Brenna had gathered this information on the pretense of taking notes for the owner regarding the garden. And she'd give those notes to Nick to pass on. But the portrait was growing more vivid each time she passed her brush over the canvas. She hoped to have it finished in time for Callie's December birthday.

The house would soon be finished, too. And Nick would move on. She kept telling herself that so she'd be prepared, so she could accept that his time here wasn't permanent. And neither was her job. They'd been working together comfortably, laughing, discussing, planning. No more kissing, though.

But every now and then, Brenna would look up and find Nick gazing at her, that intense expression pouring over his face. And she'd remember their kiss.

She stood staring out the windows now, wishing she could paint another picture. In that portrait, she'd be dancing in Nick's arms again. And this time, she'd be the sweetheart bride in the picture.

Another week had rolled by, but the image of her own wedding wouldn't leave Brenna's mind. Because it had rained off and on all week, she'd at least been spared seeing Nick every day. They'd mostly talked on the phone and through emails.

About work. About the weather. About sports. About food and movies and television. About her past, but never about his past.

Now she was in her room at home, doing a little more work on Callie's portrait. It was still a secret between Alma and Brenna. And painting had become her escape from her feelings for Nick.

Her cell phone rang, scaring Brenna. When she saw Nick's name pop up, she stared at the rain outside her window and took a deep breath. Why was he calling on a Saturday? "Hello," she said on a caught breath of guilt.

"You sound winded."

"I was…busy." For some reason, she wanted to tell him about the painting. "I…I've been painting again. I've gone out to Fleur House the last couple of Sundays to paint in the sunroom."

He chuckled. "The walls or a picture?"

She giggled. "A portrait. Of Callie."

He went silent. "A portrait of your sister?"

"Yes. I hope you don't mind—"

"No, no. I'm glad you're painting again."

Something in his voice caught at Bree's heart. Did he miss painting? Did he resent her or did he wish he could do the same?

"Nick?"

"Maybe this a bad time, then?"

Why? she wanted to shout. Not sure what to do or say, she rambled on. "No, no. I'm at home now. Just finishing up, adding hues and strokes here and there. I'm going to wash my brushes, then go back online to do some more preliminary searches for some sculptures and mixed media. Your aunt gave me some good ideas on how to coordinate things. I've found several paintings and fixtures that might work. I've explored primitives—Clementine Hunter to be specific— and I thought I'd see what kind of Southwestern art I can find."

"Good, good."

She waited, her heart beating a questioning thump. He didn't seem interested or inclined to ask her about the famous Louisiana artist who'd painted scenes of plantation life with a primitive but poignant flair.

"Did you need anything?" she finally asked.

"Well, I'm at the café, working. I called my office in San Antonio, just to check in. I have to make a run over there to clear up a complication with another project."

"Oh, okay. We'll hold down the fort here. When do you leave?"

"Tomorrow, but Brenna, I was wondering if you'd like to go with me. We'd be there a day or two at the most."

Brenna was so surprised that she couldn't speak for a full minute. How was she supposed to adhere to their work rules when the man had just asked her to go on a trip with him?

"Brenna?"

"I'm here. Just thinking."

He didn't speak for a couple of heartbeats, then finally said, "I know it's last minute, but it is strictly business. You can check out some of the galleries there, see what you think. And Tia Serena can meet us there. It makes sense for us to get with her to see what she's come up with so far."

Brenna doubted she'd be able to think clearly, let alone buy any art. "That does sound interesting."

And what timing because she'd planned to look at more art online later today, anyway.

"If you can't make it—"

"I…I can. Let me shift some things around. What time tomorrow?"

"I can wait until after church. I know how important that is to you."

Touched that he'd accepted that, she smiled to herself. "Okay. Are we driving?" Because several hours in a car with him just might do her in for good.

"No, we'll fly over to save time. I can book two tickets after we hang up. And two rooms, of course. Oh, and I'll have to drop in and see my parents while we're there, but you don't need to go with me. Unless you want to, of course. My mother wants to meet you. Tia Serena has apparently praised you."

Flying to San Antonio with Nick Santiago. And possibly meeting his family. Her day had sure changed in a hurry. "That's so nice. I wouldn't want to disappoint them, but I'd love to meet them, too. That's fine."

After telling him bye, she thought about it. "Well, I've been on other trips such as this, with other co-workers. So why are my palms all sweaty?" And why was her heart doing that rolling-over thing in her chest?

Was this really a business trip or Nick's way of pushing things between them to a new level? It might also be a good opportunity for him to tell her more about his past. And his little sister.

"I'm not so sure I like you going off with dis man."

Brenna leaned down to hug her papa's neck. "I'll be fine. It's business. I've traveled for business many, many times."

Papa bobbed his head, his thick neck red from years in the sun, his ruddy cheeks puffing in disapproval. His accent thickened with each word. "But I didn't have to know about those times, *chère*. Now I get images in my head that don't want to go away."

Brenna got some images in her head each time she thought about Nick, too. "Papa, honestly, you have to trust me. I'm a grown woman."

"I know that, but den so does he, *belle*."

"I have to go," she said on a gentle note. "And I can't be late. I'm meeting him at the house in a couple of hours and we'll drive to the New Orleans airport from there. Our flight leaves at three."

"Are you attending worship first?"

"Yes, of course. And if you don't quit giving me

the third degree so I can finish getting dressed, we'll be late for that, too."

Papa got up, his face as gray and hardened as a majestic cypress tree. "Don't get how some high-faluting stranger can come into town and start ordering everyone around."

"I thought you liked Nick," Brenna said, her hands on her hips.

Her papa mimicked her by putting his beefy hands on his own hips. "I did until I saw the way he looks at you."

Brenna sat up front with her sisters in their usual church pew, located beside a beautiful fleur-de-lis stained-glass window her family had donated to the church in her mother's memory.

She was dressed in a bright green wool skirt and a white blouse with a cozy brown-and-green tinged sweater. Her boots today were slouchy but high-heeled. She'd put on a pair of brown tights to keep her legs warm. A cold front had come through last night, but the weatherman was predicting a warm turn and possibly more storms later this week. She never could plan her wardrobe around Louisiana weather. But she'd checked the San Antonio weather forecast online and found it would warm there this week. So she'd packed lightweight slacks and a dress and a matching wrap.

Other than that, she didn't know what to expect.

She'd argued with herself all day and night about her rationale for agreeing to go on this trip. Nick was her boss and he'd asked her to go, she needed to shop for art objects for the house and she wanted to get to know Nick better.

She kept remembering that she also wanted to know what had happened to his sister. Would his family talk about that? Probably not in front of a stranger.

Brenna wondered why she had to have such a curious personality. And why did it matter so much?

While Brenna stared at the window with the purple Louisiana iris shaped like a true fleur-de-lis centered in the frame with other flowers in colors of red and orange and yellow surrounding it, a whisper started up in the back of the church and weaved its way to her pew. Then her sisters started whispering and glancing around.

Curious as always, Brenna looked back to see what all the fuss was about.

Nick Santiago strolled up the aisle, his gaze on her, his smile soft and sure and intact. And he didn't stop walking until he'd found her pew. Then he whispered "Excuse me" to the bevy of church ladies staring in awe and appreciation at him and slipped into the pew and sat down beside Brenna.

"Hi," he said, as if sitting down next to her in church was a normal, everyday occurrence.

"Hello," she said, asking it more as a question than a statement. "What are you doing?"

He looked confused, but that smile was intact. "Well, I'm attending church. Is that allowed?"

"Of course. It's just that—"

"I thought it would save time," he replied, clearly trying to dismiss her surprise. And maybe her hope, too.

"That does make sense."

"I try to be sensible."

Papa glared down the aisle at them as the organist cranked up things with "Love Lifted Me." Everyone stood and started singing. Nick stood but looked lost, so she handed him her hymnal and pointed to the verses. He nodded in appreciation but he didn't sing. He seemed to be reading the words. When the song was over, Reverend Guidry announced greeting time.

"We say hello and hug each other," she explained to Nick. When was the last time the man had darkened any church doors? Or been hugged in Christian love for that matter?

"Okay," he said, grabbing her up into his arms. "Good morning." He hugged her nice and tight and held on long enough for her to really start enjoying herself. Then he let her go but kept his hands on her elbows and his eyes on her. "I think I like church."

Shocked, Brenna stepped back and patted her ponytail. "Good morning to you, too."

Beside her, Callie elbowed her in the ribs. "When's my turn?"

Nick grinned and kissed Callie on the cheek. "Hi."

"Glad you came," Callie said, laughing.

Then Nick reached around the sisters and shook Papa's hand. "Morning, Mr. Blanchard."

"Morning to you, too," Papa said, his voice vibrating with questions and quibbles.

Afraid her daddy would start interrogating Nick right then and there, Brenna steered Nick toward Alma and Julien. "And you've met my other sister, Alma. Have you met her husband, Julien?"

"Pierre's older brother," Nick replied, shaking Julien's hand. "Nice to meet you. Your brother speaks highly of you."

"Does he now?" Julien asked, grinning. "There was a time when he sure didn't."

"Brothers tend to be that way," Nick replied.

Brenna noticed the dark sadness haunting his eyes. Was he thinking of his sister? Did he wish for a brother?

Nick and Julien went on to talk about Fleur House while Brenna greeted several other people sitting nearby. All of the ladies wanted to know about her "new boyfriend."

"He's not my boyfriend. He's my boss."

But it was useless to try and explain. Let them think what they wanted. She didn't care. Nick was her boss. Nothing more.

But she couldn't help but think about more.

In fact, she thought about a lot of things during the service. Most of them involving Nick Santiago. But she did pray in earnest. Mostly about Nick Santiago.

Before she knew it, the last hymn had been sung and everyone was leaving the sanctuary. By now, she'd worked herself up into a nervous frenzy, wondering if she should go with Nick or just stay home. If this trip involved more hugging, she was in for a whole bushel of trouble.

"Are you ready?" he asked as everyone filed out onto the parking lot. "We can grab lunch in New Orleans before the flight, if that's okay."

Brenna glanced around. Her sisters had abandoned her again, so she couldn't get one of them to take her car. She'd have to leave it parked at the church. "Uh, I guess. Sure. I need to get my bag out of my car."

"You don't sound so sure," Nick replied, his hand cupping her elbow as he took the bag she lifted out of her trunk and then walked her to his car. "Having second thoughts?"

Brenna wouldn't chicken out. That wouldn't be professional. She waited until he'd settled the stuffed bag into the trunk of his GTO. At least he'd left the old work truck he sometimes drove at the construction site. "It's just people are whispering and talking. They think we're an item or something."

Nick laughed at that. "Let 'em talk. Besides, it's really none of their business, is it?"

"Try telling the church ladies that," she replied, watching as he helped her into the car and shut the door.

Nick got in and smiled over at her. "I see what you mean. We have an audience."

"Always." She glanced in the passenger-side mirror and saw a group of older ladies laughing and pointing. "That should keep them busy for a few days. They saw you put my overnight bag in the trunk, so obviously they can see that we're headed out of town together." She'd call Callie and have her park the car at her house, at least.

He looked at the rearview mirror. "Would that ruin your reputation?"

She turned back and stared straight ahead. "No more than it's already ruined. They know I broke up with Jeffrey and lost my job all in the same week. They sure know I'm living with Papa out on the bayou. Now, they'll have a field day discussing this."

"It's a business trip," he said. He must have been

practicing that explanation a lot, too. "Want to ride by and shout that out the window?"

"Oh, never mind," Brenna retorted. "Let's just go."

Nick cranked the car and turned out of the parking lot. "I enjoyed the service."

Surprised, Brenna glanced over at him. "Good. I'm glad you came. I wasn't expecting you, but I'm glad you came all the same."

He shot her a black-eyed glance. "Worried about my soul, Brenna?"

She didn't want to preach him another sermon because they'd just heard a good one about second chances and walking within the light. Nick could certainly use some of that light of the gospel. She was worried, but she held out hope. "No, I'm just happy that you decided to come to church. I think you impressed Papa."

"Good. I respect your daddy, that's for sure."

"He's not as overbearing and snarly as he lets on."

"And neither are you."

She had to laugh at that. Sitting back, she relaxed a little now that they had reached the city limits sign. "I'm sorry if I seemed silly back there. It's hard sometimes, living in a small community. Everyone knows your business and what they don't know, they tend to make up."

"I understand that. My parents have neighbors

who are like that. I guess it's human nature to want to gossip and speculate." His eyes went into that dark mode.

"Yes. They're good people, but they seem to love matchmaking."

He gave another one of those rich, dark stares. "We wouldn't be such a bad match, would we?"

Floored, Brenna didn't know how to respond. The man needed to make up his mind about things. Finally she said, "I'm thinking we don't need to go down that road. Work, Nick. We need to focus on work. I can't wait to explore some of the galleries along the River Walk in San Antonio."

"Right," he said, his eyes on the road. "Because my meetings are downtown, you'll be able to explore all you want."

Brenna was glad to hear that. If he stayed busy with his meetings, she could get more of her work done. "Sounds like a good plan."

"In the meantime," he said with a nod, "w have a few hours together on this trip. And no on else around to gossip about what we say. A goo chance to really get to know each other."

Brenna realized too late that she hadn't factor in the long day alone with Nick. What should t talk about? Would he finally tell her what had h pened with his sister? She'd resisted going b

to the article she'd found. Or rather, she'd felt too guilty to look again.

Somehow, she had to make Nick see that he could trust her. Maybe if she opened up more, so would he. After all, he'd ventured into church this morning. That meant his heart might be calling to the Lord.

Or maybe his heart was only calling to her heart.

Either way, it was a first step toward what she hoped would bring about a new relationship with God and a new beginning in Nick's faith journey.

She could help with that. She wanted to help with that.

And she truly wanted to help him heal from the grief of losing a loved one. After all, she knew all about that sort of grief.

Chapter Thirteen

They had lunch at a greasy spoon near the airport. Country vegetables for Brenna and corn bread with peppered steak and mashed potatoes for Nick.

"Very good," Nick commented after they were back in the car. "Did you enjoy your food?"

Brenna rubbed her tummy. "I think so. I'm stuffed. I don't usually eat that much in one sitting."

"You seemed nervous." He waited a beat. "Is that because of me?"

She had to smile at that. So far, the chatter between them had been mostly small talk mixed in with discussing Fleur House. She hadn't gotten very far in her you-need-to-trust-me quest to make Nick open up. But she wasn't giving up.

"No. I mean maybe. Yes, okay, you make me nervous."

"Because I'm the big bad boss?"

"No, because you're…you." He gave her a Nick-glance, full of mystery and promise. "That—that right there makes me nervous."

He held his hands out, palms up. "What?"

"The way you look at me."

"I like looking at you, okay?"

"Okay. Let's change the subject."

"Let's get back to you eating. You manage to stay healthy in spite of all the pie and bread pudding you eat."

"My family loves to eat, what can I say?" she retorted. "We do try to eat healthy now and then. And for the most part, we are all healthy." It was her turn to go to dark memories.

"You're thinking about your mother, right?"

She nodded. "That and the threat of cancer for all of us."

He looked ahead at the road. "That must be hard to live with."

"It is, but then death and grief are not easy subjects for any of us."

She watched in amazement as he let that opening slide away.

His gaze skimmed her face, a look close to a plea centered in his expression. "I don't mean to… I mean, you don't seem to have any problems with that. You look like you're in great shape, so I hope you're taking care of yourself."

"I have regular checkups and mammograms,"

she replied, wishing there was a medical test for people who closed down in their grief.

"And you seem to get lots of exercise."

"I love to walk," she admitted, ignoring what she was pretty sure must have been his attempt at a compliment. "I used to walk everywhere in downtown Baton Rouge. I'd walk at the indoor track at the gym near my condo, too."

"I've seen you walking around the gardens at Fleur House," he replied. "I do that sometimes early in the morning. I like to jog when I have the time."

She pictured him up and out and running, running, his thoughts focused on what he needed to accomplish.

"Is that your thinking time?"

"I guess it is. That and late at night when I can't sleep."

"I do that." She found it endearing that they had some of the same habits at least. "I get a thought in my head and then I'm wide-awake."

"Same here." He didn't speak for a few minutes. "I've always been a loner. I don't need much sleep, so I do get a lot done. I like my quiet time."

Brenna wondered about that. She wanted to ask him why he no longer painted. But then he might figure out she'd seen that picture of Jessica on the internet. "Don't you ever get lonely?"

He took a deep breath and adjusted his foot on the gas pedal. "Sure. At times. Who doesn't?"

She catalogued that information and went head-first into another question. "You don't seem to have much of a life outside of your work. I don't mean to sound condemning, but don't you get tired of traveling from place to place, rebuilding, then leaving all over again?"

His chuckle rumbled through the car. "I never have before," he said, glancing over at her. "But now I'm beginning to wonder about that."

Brenna was too shocked to say anything else. The way he'd looked at her just now made her feel all soft and warm and confused. "What makes you wonder?"

"You," he said, his expression full of questions. "I thought that kiss might cure me of wondering, but I'm afraid it just made things worse."

Now they were getting down to the real business. She sat up against the seat. "I don't want to make things worse for you, Nick. Why did you ask me on this trip? Really, really ask me. We both know I can find what I need in New Orleans or anywhere in the world for that matter, and you certainly didn't need me for your meeting."

He slowed the car as they approached the busy Louis Armstrong International Airport, then glanced over at her again. "You're right. I didn't need you to come on this trip with me. But I wanted you with me all the same."

"I don't get it," Brenna admitted. "What's going on here?"

"That's what I'm trying to find out."

"Oh, so first you kiss me to find out what's going on and you try to get me off your mind. Now, you invited me on a road trip to test that theory even more?"

"Yeah, something like that."

"You're an interesting, confusing man."

"And you're a challenging, confusing woman."

"This is gonna be one mighty strange trip."

He touched his hand to hers. "Or it could turn out to be the best trip of our lives."

Brenna liked the whisper of a promise in his words.

But she still wanted him to open up to her, to trust her, to share the worst he had with her. She'd let Jeffrey slide by on the intimacy issues and look where that had gotten her—alone and heartbroken. She hadn't pushed enough with her ex. Or maybe she'd pushed too much. It didn't matter. Things were different with Nick. She liked him. A lot. So she wanted to be his friend and his confidante. She wanted him to know he had her in his corner and that God was right there with them.

But she wasn't so sure he was ready for that. And she had to wonder what kind of test he'd put her through before he would be willing to offer her more.

Surprising her yet again, he reached for her hand. "Brenna, promise me you'll take care of yourself."

And then she suddenly understood a lot more about the man beside her. He wasn't afraid of getting involved with a woman. He was afraid of falling for *her*. Because of her family history with cancer. And because he had already lost someone he loved.

Brenna held on to his hand. "I'm fine, Nick. You don't have to worry about me."

But he did. She could see it in his eyes before he let go of her hand.

Nick adjusted his seat and prepared for the flight. "Not long now," he said. "Just a few hours and we'll be there."

He wondered now if he'd been wise to bring Brenna with him. He'd stepped over a big boundary, telling her that he wanted to get her out of his mind. Telling her one thing and then doing another could only confuse her even more. And him, too.

He could admit it now, at least. He wanted Brenna in his life, but his fear of a lasting commitment crippled his clumsy attempts at making that happen. He'd had enough grief and loss in his life. Loving someone for a lifetime was asking more of him than he could bear.

"Where is our hotel?" Brenna asked, her head down as she stared out the plane's window.

Nick worried with his seat belt. "It's on the River Walk."

"Oh, that's convenient."

He grinned, glad to have something else besides his erratic, irrational fears to think about. "*Sí*. But, we have to go by and see my parents first. I can't go to San Antonio and not visit with my parents. They'd never forgive me."

"Okay." She squirmed and fidgeted, her big eyes touching on him before she glanced away.

"You don't have to go with me. I could drop you off at the hotel first."

"I don't mind," she replied. "I'd love to meet your family."

"You don't look too excited about it, though." He put a hand on hers. "All you have to do is relax and enjoy the next couple of days away from Fleur. We'll be home Tuesday morning and you'll be fine."

Wiggling, she adjusted her seat belt again. "I don't know your family. What if they don't like me? I guess I'm a little overwhelmed."

He tilted his head toward her. "I want you to get to know them. And they're already asking about you."

"But they don't know me, either. How could they ask questions?"

"My Tia Serena gave them a glowing report. That's why they insisted I come by the house. My mom wouldn't have it any other way."

She shook her head. "Aren't we just fueling the fire all over again? They don't think we're an item, do they?"

"Not that I can tell, but I'm sure Tia Serena thinks we should be an item. So that means she's probably convinced the whole family, too."

Looking perturbed, Brenna gave him a light tap on his arm. "Is this another part of getting me out of your system? So you asked me here to test me on your parents?"

He couldn't hide his frown. "Well, when you put it that way—"

"Are you serious?" She glanced toward the front of the plane. "I have a good mind to get off this plane and go home."

Maybe she could bolt from a moving plane, after all.

"I'm teasing," he said to cover his worry. "I've explained that we work together. Nothing more."

"Good. Let's keep it that way."

"Fine. You'll only have to endure them for dinner tonight. Tomorrow, it's all business."

She gave him a skeptical glare. "I sure hope so."

Nick put his head back on the seat. He'd never

brought a woman home before, especially not a woman who worked with him. And he'd worked with lots of beautiful women. Why was Brenna so different? Why did she make his heart do too much pumping? Why did she make him *want* to settle down and stick around?

And why did he keep her so close when he knew he should push her away? Anyone with a brain could see he'd purposely brought her on this business trip just so he could be with her. But would it hurt to have a little fun with a pretty woman, a woman he admired and appreciated? Already, she's helped him with several problems regarding Fleur House. She was good at her job and she was good at spotting issues.

Maybe that was why she sat with a tight-lipped pout right now. She had discovered an issue with his methods of trying to woo her. Maybe he should just level with her and get it over and done with, tell her he was a coward and he couldn't handle anything more than friendship and working together.

"Brenna?"

"What?"

"I should have told you…about going to see my parents right away. I'm sorry."

"Okay, all right. You did tell me they wanted to meet me. Might as well get to that right up front. I'll be fine. Really."

The plane lifted in the air. At least she was still sitting there. "Looks like the weather will be great," he said, trying to make small talk.

She stared out the window. "Wonderful. Can't wait."

Nick took her hand again. "Now, *bonita,* don't be mad at me. I wanted to extend a bit of hospitality to you. You'll like my family. We're very close, but they tend to be stifling at times. They mean well, but they can't see that I'm a grown man."

She finally turned to look at him. "I can see that and so much more about you. Just like my family. Our mother's death brought all of us closer together. Then Callie got cancer and well…it's hard sometimes. I worry—"

His heart hit turbulence even though the takeoff had been smooth. "That it might happen to you?"

"Yes." Her eyes turned a rich greenish-brown. "Yes. It's hard on a relationship, so I can understand your being hesitant. Jeffrey always laughed off my worries about breast cancer, but then, he laughed off a lot of my concerns."

Nick's heart ached for what she'd been through. He knew that same ache. It tore through him each time he thought of his beautiful little sister. Before he could stop himself, he said, "Jessica's death changed all of us. Part of my soul is broken, always raw."

Brenna's expression softened, her pout disappearing as quickly as it had come. "I'm so sorry. You said you don't like to talk about her, but Nick, I understand that kind of grief. It's blinding and hard to shake. And it makes getting close to people even harder." She waited, the expectation in her pretty eyes bright with hope and that gentle understanding she'd mentioned. "I think I have that same little tear in my soul. Maybe that's why Jeffrey only pretended to love me. Maybe because I only pretended to love him."

Nick wanted to tell her everything, but he'd been silent on this subject for so long that he couldn't bring himself to reveal his feelings, even to Brenna. "We'd better get back to business for now, don't you think?"

Disappointment shadowed the hope he'd seen in her eyes. "Okay. You're right, of course. And I need to stop being pushy."

He didn't respond at first, but he didn't want to leave things this way when they'd started out. "About Jeffrey, maybe you needed him to love you more—enough so that your feelings and fears wouldn't be so hard to handle."

"Yes," she said, giving him one of her daring gazes. "That's the kind of love I want. Someone who helps me through the bad stuff instead of dismissing my feelings as irrational or unreal. Someone who can overcome fear to experience love, real love that fights through good and bad." She gave him a brief glance, then turned back to the window. "Yes, that's what I want."

Nick thought about her words. How would she feel if he ever did tell her the whole story about his sister? He never talked about that subject, not even with his own family. But he knew one thing: if his feelings for Brenna were as real as they seemed, he'd never let cancer or heartache or any pain come her way again. Never. And he'd need to be completely honest with her, too, or he'd lose her.

"I think we all want that kind of love," he finally said.

She sat there, staring over at him, her expression shifting in shades of sunlight and white-washed clouds and finally, she smiled. "I can't wait to meet your family."

Chapter Fourteen

The Santiago home was settled on a nice cul-de-sac in an older neighborhood full of trees and pretty landscaping. The house was stucco and two-storied with an inviting front porch and Spanish-style arches that reminded Brenna of Fleur House. Palm trees and old oaks surrounded the shaded yard.

Brenna took in the big house, her mind still reeling from their earlier conversation. He'd come so close to sharing his pain with her. Maybe if she kept gently prodding, she'd know the truth one day, but she was thankful she'd finally figured out part of his hesitation toward her. She said a tiny prayer, asking God to give her patience to wait and to give Nick the strength to trust her. What kind of pain had he held inside his heart all this time? So much that he couldn't let go and find someone to love?

"This is it—my parents' home," Nick said, his eyes shining with pride. And something else. Regret, maybe?

Brenna gave him a quick smile. "It's beautiful. So peaceful and neat."

"My dad loves puttering in the garden." He opened his door. "Ready for this?"

"As ready as I'll ever be." Brenna opened her door and hopped out of the rental car. "The weather forecast was right. It is warmer here."

"Just a little. It can get warm and humid, even in fall and winter. It's a lot like Louisiana."

"Then I was smart to pack a variety of clothes."

He gathered their bags and guided her up the curving walkway to the front door. But before they'd made it halfway, several people fell out the door, all talking at once in Spanish.

"They're discussing how pretty you are," Nick explained with a grin.

Brenna stepped back as a voluptuous woman grabbed Nick and held him tight. She heard the word *bebé* and figured this must be Nick's mother.

"And this must be your lovely Brenna," the woman said, her hands reaching out to Brenna. "Welcome to our home."

"Hi," Brenna said before she was engulfed in a strong hug. A mother's hug. Brenna clung tight and savored the feeling, memories of her mother's soothing touch coloring the confusion hovering over her brain. "You're Nick's mom?"

"Yes, *sí*. Jeanette," the woman said. She smelled of cinnamon and wore her gray-streaked dark hair up in a beautiful silver clip. "And this is my husband, Alberto."

"Nice to meet you," the man said to Brenna.

"Hi, Dad," Nick said, shaking his father's hand.

Even though his hair was almost white, the older man looked a lot like Nick and seemed just as stoic and quiet, too. "Nicky, good to have you home. And to bring us such a pretty *chiquita,* too. We are honored."

Brenna was then shepherded around and introduced to the other people who'd come out to greet them. Aunts and uncles and cousins and long-lost relatives. Apparently, Nick's coming home was a big deal. Or had they all come to inspect her?

When they finally got through the front door, she glanced up to view the rest of the house and was happy to see Tia Serena coming down the wide staircase.

The older lady, elegant and graceful, took Brenna by the arm. "You're here. I'm so glad. I think they invited the whole family, and Nick, your papa has grilled and cooked right along with Jeanette. Hope you're both hungry."

Brenna grinned as Serena swept both of them close and kissed them each on the cheek. "I asked him to bring you on this trip, so don't be angry. I wanted us to get some preliminary work done and I wanted everyone to meet you."

Brenna shot a quick glance at Nick. He hadn't told her Serena had requested her. He obviously wanted her here, but the mystery of what motivated him held her. He seemed happy, but she could still see that darkness in his eyes. "I'm not angry," she replied to Serena. "Just a little intimidated."

"We tend to do that to people," Serena explained. "But I'm here to filter things and keep everyone from poking too hard at you, *si?*"

"I appreciate that," Brenna said, meaning it. Normally, she didn't mind being the center of attention, but this was Nick. This was different. She couldn't forget that this man seemed to have a process—a method to his madness. He'd brought her here for some reason and it involved more than work. It rankled, but she wanted to pass inspection. She thought about Jeffrey and how she'd tried to pass muster with him.

This is different, she told herself. With Jeffrey, passing included wearing the right clothes and knowing the right people, things that would move them up the all-important corporate and social ladders. Passing Nick's test was all about gaining trust and unlocking the secrets he held in his heart.

Wondering if she'd ever get an A-plus in the love department, Brenna said a silent little prayer. *Only with You, Lord. That's where it counts.*

Serena's calming voice lifted over the chatter. "Nicky, show Brenna where to freshen up. We will have a good supper waiting when you come down."

"Okay." Nick finished hugging and kissing everyone. Motioning to Brenna, he said, "I'll show the bathroom upstairs. You'll have more privacy there."

Nick took Brenna upstairs without a word. When they reached the second door on the right, he pointed to it. "The bigger, quieter bathroom, as promised. I'll be downstairs."

Then he turned and headed down without another word.

Now she really felt uncomfortable. Was he angry that so many people had come to see him? Or was he mad that his family had made the wrong assumption. Brenna wanted to run downstairs and call a cab to take her back to the airport. She cared about Nick a lot, wanted to get to know him better, but this was almost too much. He'd brought her on this trip because according to him, he wanted her here.

But did he also bring her here so she could see his big, happy family? So she'd stop pestering him or trying to turn him back on the right path? Or to scare her away?

His entire family seemed to be a happy, carefree lot and yet, he seemed so tragic and sad at times. And to top it all off, she'd have to put on a good front and go with the questions and assumption. What was going on?

After she'd combed her hair and put on fresh lipstick, Brenna walked out into the hallway, her gaze falling on the room directly across from the upstairs bathroom.

A real girly-girl room.

Glancing around while she stood outside the door, she saw family pictures here and there and recognized Nick in them. And Jessica. Brenna leaned close to search a large family portrait. A skinny young girl sat with her arm over Nick's shoulder, her smile beaming and bright.

Jessica. And yes, this Jessica certainly looked like the girl she'd caught a glimpse of in that newspaper article.

"What are you doing?"

Her hand on the wall, Brenna whirled to find Nick standing on the stairs, glaring at her.

"I'm sorry. I…I couldn't help but notice—"

His expression changed from angry to miserable and embarrassed. "My family means well, but they're trying to make a point with me. They kept this room as some sort of shrine to my sister and they always make sure I remember it's still here."

Brenna didn't know what to say. "It's hard to let go. You saw the portrait of my mother over our mantel. I think it's okay to keep mementoes and photos of lost loved ones."

"*Si.* I saw the portrait of your mother, but I didn't see a whole room dedicated to her memory."

"No, we have a whole house that's filled with memories of her. We remember her each and every day."

"But you don't force those memories. They're natural and true and pure."

"I think so. We…we loved her, so we celebrate her life and we rejoice that she's with God now."

He came to stand with her, but he didn't look into the room. "I haven't gotten over Jessica's death. I don't think I ever will, but they push and push and try to make everything bright and happy. It's a facade for my sake. After I leave, they go back to their quiet suffering."

"While you're still suffering out there alone?"

He nodded, lowered his head. "I haven't been in here since she died. The door is usually closed."

"But why would they want to force you to come in her room if it bothers you?"

He held her, his hands on her elbows. "They love me. I know that. So they think they can make everything better, even after all these years. They have such a strong faith. It isn't as hard for them to keep going." He looked into Brenna's eyes, his expression begging her to understand. "If I can stand here with you, then I can go on with my life—that's what they are hoping."

Brenna didn't stop to think. She pulled him into her arms and hugged him close. "Nick, grief takes many forms and it's a process that works differently for every person. I can close the door for you." And open another door on hope, she thought.

"No, no." He pulled away but held her there. "I'm okay, really. Seeing you here, having you understand, has helped me a lot." He searched her face. "Sometimes, turning to a more objective person does help."

"I can be that person," she replied. "Whatever happened when Jessica died, I can be that person for you, Nick. Between God and me, you can heal."

"Did God help you when your mother died?"

"Yes," she said, touched that he was willing to discuss this. "Yes, my faith, my family's strong faith, got us through. Because we know, no matter our suffering here on earth, we'll see our mother one day again—in heaven. You have to trust in that, too."

He touched his forehead to hers. "Heaven seems so far away. So far."

Brenna looked up, saw the torment in his eyes and wondered why the good Lord had commissioned her to be this man's spiritual guidance counselor. She wasn't qualified but she wouldn't turn away, either. "Heaven is far away, but God is close. He's always right here." She touched a hand to Nick's heart and felt the erratic beating. It reminded her of a trapped bird trying to break free.

Nick put his hand over hers and stared down at her. "You're an amazing person."

Brenna felt humbled by his words. "Not really. I'm just a very determined person. And I'm determined to make you smile again. I mean really smile."

She pulled away and lifted her hand to encompass the neat girly-girl room. "This is part of heaven. You have memories, people smiling and laughing together, Jessica's favorite things all around. This is what you hold on to, Nick."

"I'd rather hold on to you," he said, grabbing her to pull her back.

Brenna gladly went into his arms. But his desperate words left her feeling deflated instead of joyful. Was he holding on to her just to ease the pain of his grief? And if so, what would happen to her if he decided to let go?

Brenna sat on an intricately carved bench out in the backyard, a giant magnolia tree shading her from the late-day sun. In spite of the warmth, she couldn't help but shiver. There was a sadness shrouding this otherwise-happy home.

Nick brought her another glass of tea and sat down beside her. "Looks like we'll get to see a brilliant sunset."

She leaned back, relaxed from the good food and all the chatter of his family. Once she'd made it back downstairs and talked with everyone, she'd felt more at ease. But she couldn't forget the way Nick had held on to her, there by his sister's room. "You're blessed, you know."

"I do know." He glanced back to where his parents and the other were inside the courtyard patio clearing away the remains of their feast. "I should come home more often."

"We all should," she replied. "I wish now that I'd had more time with my mother."

He looked down at his hands. "Same here. I imagine Jessica all grown up and beautiful. I'd probably test all of her prom dates for perfection."

"The way you're testing me?" she asked, trying to keep things light.

His head shot up. "Do you really think that's what I'm doing?"

"Aren't you?" She set her glass down in the soft grass, then turned to him. "You seem to have a method to all your actions."

"I do have a process for work," he admitted, "but when it comes to you—"

"You're using the same process. Kissing me to see where it would go, inviting me here to see how it would be having me around your family." Not to mention, still not telling her anything about what had happened to his sister. Not mentioning that his aunt also wanted her to visit. She needed him to be up front and honest with her. Maybe that would be the real test. "What's next for me?"

He took her hand in his. "I don't know. And I didn't deliberately plan all of my actions. I think things through, long and hard, before I make any kind of move. I guess I'm doing that with you, too."

"Serena said she also wanted me on this trip, but you never mentioned that."

He looked surprised. "Does it matter? I asked you to come and I am your direct supervisor."

"Oh, we're gonna play it like that now?" She shifted, stared off into the sunset. "Nick, I understand this is business and I'll do my part. But we both know this is also personal. Are you and your family so desperate that you'd parade me around like some prize?"

He stood and stared down at her. "No one here intended to make you feel as if you were on exhibit, Brenna."

"No, no. You've all been kind and wonderful,

but there is a weird dynamic here. Your family is so different from mine."

He sat back down, let out a long sigh. "So you noticed?"

"Um, yes. But I can tell there's a lot of love here, too. You should focus on that. And you should learn to rely on your friends a little bit more."

He nodded, took her hand in his. "I'm not so good at that and I'm truly sorry for how this might look." He stared down at their joined fingers. "The bottom line is I really wanted you here with me. I'm sorry for everything else."

Brenna could see the sincerity in his eyes. "I don't mind so much as long as you're honest with me," she replied, her hand squeezing his. "And if you can learn to trust me."

"Ah, trust." He looked over his shoulder. "Everyone tells me I should trust and let go. That's a tall order for someone who has to program every step."

"You have to see things to believe in them?"

He looked into her eyes. "Yes. I see you sitting here and I believe I need to keep you around."

She laughed at that, and used his previous words. "Well, when you put it that way."

He groaned, then pushed a hand through his inky hair. "Tomorrow, after work, I want to take you to a special place."

"Dinner?"

"No, but you won't go hungry. It's the *hacienda pequeña*—my home when I'm back here for long periods."

His little hacienda. "Your one true home?"

"As close to a home as I've had since I left home."

Brenna didn't know what to say. Nick taking her to such a private, personal place. Another test?

But she wouldn't say no. She wanted to see the little house she'd heard so much about. "That sounds nice. I'd love to see it."

Maybe he was beginning to trust her, after all. First, the family and now a place where he could be alone and away from everyone and everything. With her.

As if he knew what she was thinking, he leaned close and whispered, "Don't worry. You know, you need to trust me a little bit, too."

He was right. And she would try.

The next morning, Serena met Brenna at the hotel bright and early to explore the River Walk. Nick told them he'd meet them later for lunch and they'd all give updates.

Getting used to his procedures now, Brenna smiled and told him goodbye.

"How did you sleep?" Serena asked, her hand on Brenna's arm as they strolled along with their fresh coffee in hand.

"Is that a trick question?" Brenna replied.

Serena's smile filled with acceptance. "Ah, so you think we are one strange family, right?"

Brenna sipped her coffee. "No, not any different from most. You're all obviously still grieving Jessica. It's not my place to judge."

Serena guided her into an art gallery. "We only want the best for Nicky. We want him happy and whole again."

"So you think you can give him the best by forcing him to stare at his sister's things left all around like a shrine?"

Serena gave Brenna a quick, appreciative glance. "You do care about my nephew."

Brenna wouldn't deny it. "Of course I do. He's a good man who obviously went through something traumatic, something that still haunts him."

"Still," Serena repeated. "It's been over fifteen years."

Fifteen years. Brenna thought about the newspaper article she'd found. That would have been the right time frame.

"What happened?" she finally asked.

Serena shook her head. "You have to let Nick tell you. He'd never forgive me if I said anything more."

Frustrated, Brenna watched tourist boats floating by on the long canal through the River Walk. "That's not fair. He brought me here for a reason other than work, but no one wants to explain the man to me. He's hurting. Can't anyone see that?"

"We all see it," Serena replied. "I helped raise that boy and I was there when the worst happened. Jessica's death was hard on everyone, but Nick took it the hardest. We all tried to help him through. But—"

"But he blames himself, right?" Brenna asked, the assumption clear in her head.

Serena didn't speak for a full minute. Then she said, "*Sí*. Nicky blames himself for his sister's death. And, unfortunately, that's all I can say on the matter."

Chapter Fifteen

The rest of the day went by in a blaze of shopping, lunch and strolling along the crowded sidewalks. Brenna loved how a canal ran through the city, complete with large gondoliers carrying tourists and locals from place to place. Serena took her to a wonderful art gallery where, using the computer-generated sketches of the layout of the house, she found some mixed-media renderings to use in a couple of bedrooms and exquisite sculpture pieces to place here and there. She asked to have the items shipped and used the company charge card Nick had given her to pay for everything.

"A good day's work," she told Serena. Nick had been unable to meet them for lunch, so after doing some shopping for themselves, they headed back toward the hotel lobby.

"I enjoyed this," Serena said, her expression calm as always. "And I enjoy working with you. You definitely have an eye for design."

Brenna basked in that compliment. "What can I say? It's the only thing I'm good at. I love to paint and I love to deal in art. I liked my job at the gallery, but it was a challenge at times."

"Have you ever considered becoming an independent art dealer?" Serena asked. "You'd be good at that."

Brenna shook her head. "No. But then, I had a good job and never considered leaving my position. I'll have to look into that. Sounds as if I could work for myself and still have a job I love."

"Exactly," Serena said. "You could travel and work wherever you want as long as you have a client list. And that wouldn't be hard at all. You'd have to do some promotion work and advertising to get your name out there. I have contacts, too, of course. I'd recommend you."

"I'd need that," Brenna replied. "I hadn't thought past Fleur House, but I probably should consider what might be next. The house is scheduled to be finished by next spring."

Serena laughed. "Nick put a rush on everything. He's determined to meet his deadlines."

"I'm sure he is," Brenna replied.

And then, he'd be gone out of her life.

She needed to consider what she'd do next, so she was grateful to Serena for making the suggestion. Brenna would need something to keep her focused so she wouldn't miss Nick so much.

* * *

"Sorry I missed lunch," Nick told her as they left the city later that afternoon and headed south. "Things got complicated and my meeting ran longer than I'd planned."

"That's okay," Brenna replied. "We managed to have fun without you."

"Good." His smile held a hint of fatigue. "It was a long day for me, but we ironed out the problems on our next project. I missed you."

Brenna fidgeted with the fringe on her white wrap, then adjusted the skirt of her blue jersey dress. "I kind of missed you, too."

He took her hand. "Just kind of?"

A lot. But she didn't tell him that. "Yes, kind of. I was busy working, you know."

"Right." He laughed and dropped her hand. "I saw all those packages piled in your room. "How will we get all of that onto the plane?"

She leaned close and grinned. "That's an old feminine secret. We know how to consolidate. It will all fit into my suitcase because I left extra room."

"Ah, so that's how it's done."

She nodded. "Throughout the centuries."

"You're amazing. A constant surprise."

"Is that a good or bad thing?"

He took her hand again. "Good. But bad for my head."

Before she could say anything, her cell phone buzzed.

"Callie, what's up?"

Her sister sounded out of breath. "Have you heard the weather report?"

"Uh, no. We were out all day. Why?"

"Remember that little tropical disturbance out in the Gulf? Well, it took a turn and regained speed and strength. Now it's headed our way."

"Wow." Brenna turned to Nick and relayed the message. "When is it due?"

"They're saying midweek at the earliest. I'm sure Nick is aware, but I just wanted to let you know what I've heard."

"I'll check the radar and see. We'll be home tomorrow, anyway, so don't fret too much."

"Okay," Callie said. "Papa is pacing and worrying. That should make him feel better, knowing you'll get home safely."

"Okay. We'll keep tabs on it."

"Hey, Brenna, tell Nick he might want to consider what to do about Fleur House. It could sustain damage if those winds get as bad as they're predicting."

Brenna glanced over at Nick. "I'm sure he's thinking about that right now."

After she put her phone away, she turned to

Nick. "A storm could wipe out a lot of the work you've already done on the house. Should we leave early tomorrow?"

He nodded. "We're almost to the hacienda. I'll start calling as soon as we pull off the highway. My foreman should know what to do, but we'll make sure all the same. I've had my eye on these approaching storms, but I didn't check today. I'm surprised he hasn't called me about this."

"I can make some calls right now," she offered. "He probably wanted to wait to make sure, but my sister didn't wait. We've been through this too many times, so she knows the drill."

Nick gave her a couple of names and numbers so she could change their flight and alert the project foreman. By the time she was finished, they'd turned into a gated driveway. Nick hit a remote and the gate swung open. He pulled up into the long dirt drive and shut off the rental car. "Let me get a couple more calls made and then I'll show you the hacienda."

"You don't seem too worried," she said, wondering how he managed to stay so calm.

"I've been through this before, too," he said. "Galveston's been through some of the same rough weather as your coastline in Louisiana. I have a lot of clients who lost their homes in the last hurricane."

She nodded, thinking he was one of the hardest-working men she'd ever met. They clicked in that respect. They both did their jobs with gusto and passion. Maybe because their work was all they had right now.

Thirty minutes later and just as the sun had begun its descent into the western sky, Nick pulled the car up to a white cottage-size house that indeed was a true miniature hacienda.

The front porch held arched columns a lot like the bigger ones at Fleur House. But this porch was more Southwestern in design, long and narrow and inviting. A red slate roof slanted down to meet the porch and palm trees and huge cactus plants graced the front yard. Off to one side, an ancient live oak stood like a sentinel, guarding the house.

"It's beautiful," Brenna said, a warmth seeping into her bones. "Timeless."

"It's close to one hundred and fifty years old," Nick said. "My great-grandparents lived here and over the years, relatives kept adding to it. It was in disrepair when it was passed to my family. I begged my dad to let me renovate it."

"Obviously, he agreed."

Nick nodded, his eyes full of that dark torment she'd seen before. "*Sí.* It was one of my first projects after I'd been away at school for a while. Took me a whole year, but I had to make sure I kept it authentic."

Brenna looked at the cozy little house, wondering if this house had helped him with some of his grief. Maybe that feeling of diving into a project had stayed with him through each home he restored. That would explain his need to keep working.

"If this was your first restoration project, I'd sure like to see some of the others. It's gorgeous."

"Gracias." He stared up at the house. "This place means a lot to me."

Brenna could understand. The house reminded her of something out of a fairy tale. She expected to see a beautiful *señorita* wearing black lace and holding a fan, waiting for them at the door. "I can't wait to see the rest."

Nick hurried around to help her out, then held her hand as they stood there for a minute. "Let's watch the sunset," he said. "It's always beautiful here, this time of day."

Brenna glanced beyond the house to the vast acreage of trees and shrubs spread across the surrounding pasture land and watched as the sun faded away in a brilliant orange-yellow glimmering glow that set off the stark white of the house and left the whole world a shimmering, glittering bronze.

"Wow."

Nick pulled her into his arms and looked her in the eye, then reached up his hand to pull at a strand of her hair. "Wow, yourself. I'm glad you're here."

"Me, too," she said. She thought he would kiss her and she almost died with frustration when instead he took her by the hand again. "Let's go inside."

The little house was cozy and clean. While the furnishings were stark and minimalist, they echoed the Southwestern theme, complete with paintings of the desert and beautiful clay pots here and there. Chunky wooden hutches, rustic tables and massive armoires mingled with rich brown leathers, handwoven looms and exquisite throw rugs. A massive iron-and-glass chandelier centered in the high ceiling brightened the whole place. The white color carried through to the inside of the house in a predominant theme and shined brightly against the severe browns in the furnishing and the rich red tiles of the floor.

Brenna looked around, taking in the decor. Then her gaze moved up the fireplace wall and she almost gasped. She glanced briefly at Nick. His gaze was centered on the portrait she'd just noticed, but he dropped his head and moved away before she could see his reaction.

The portrait of Jessica she'd briefly glimpsed on the internet was hanging over the fireplace. She almost said something, but she didn't want to disrupt the closeness she felt toward Nick. Maybe he would explain the portrait. Had he brought her here for that reason?

Right now, he was preoccupied with turning on lights and lighting candles.

While Brenna wandered around the big open living room and absorbed yet another revelation, Nick lit a fire in the arched kiva fireplace, then turned to smile at her. "Are you hungry? I called ahead and had one of the ranch hands bring down some cheese and fruit. And I have coffee or soda."

"That would be nice," she said, not sure what to do. "Coffee sounds wonderful. It's chilly now that the sun's gone down."

"Come stand by the fire," he said. "I'll get us something to eat."

Brenna walked across toward the fireplace and put her back to the growing flames. The kitchen was tucked in one corner, neat and bright with colorful blue tiles across the backsplash. She watched Nick prepare the coffee and food and then she sat down on the tiled ledge in front of the fireplace.

"You must love coming here. It's so quiet and peaceful."

Nick brought over a tray with coffee and their food, then took a seat by her. "*Sí.* It's nice to get away and relax, even if I only do it on rare occasions. The stars are a lot brighter out in this big pasture."

She nibbled on a few grapes and speared a chunk of white cheddar. "You mentioned a ranch hand. Is this a working ranch?"

He nodded. "My father still comes out here once or twice a week to oversee things. This land has been in my family for a long, long time. We used to love to come out and ride horses or just have a barbecue and relax—my parents and relatives still do that a lot. Our workers have their own homes on the land, so it's a good place for all of us."

"Why did your parents move into the city?"

His face went blank, like a shutter blocking out the light. He looked up at the portrait above the fireplace. "It was hard being here...after Jessica died."

Stunned, Brenna stared at him. "Is that her in the picture?"

He kept staring at the portrait. "Yes."

No explanation.

Brenna scrambled for the right thing to say. "But Jessica has a room at the house in the city."

He nodded. "That's why it's such a bone of contention between my parents and me. They set up that room when they moved there."

Brenna's heart ached for this family. "Nick, your parents are good people. Don't they see that this hurts you?"

He took a breath. "They only see a young girl frozen in life. She'll always be fifteen to them. I don't mind the room so much, but I do mind that they seem to want me to grieve in the same way they do. I can't. I won't. I will never stop grieving, but they expect me to let God heal me. They try to force the issue and I bolt every time."

"It makes you uncomfortable?"

"It makes me angry. Jessica shouldn't have died."

"No, but then, we don't get to make that choice."

His gaze hit against hers. "No, we don't. But God does. And I don't understand why."

Brenna knew she was treading on shaky ground. Explaining God's grace to someone who'd lost a loved one wasn't easy. No amount of words or platitudes could help that. And hadn't she felt the same when her mother died?

"You have a picture of her here, though."

"I do. I painted that picture. It's the only thing I have left of her. I know she's gone, but they...they seem to think she's still around. I don't like it."

Brenna tried to gently reason with him. "Maybe your way of dealing with it is not the same as how they handle things. They might be acknowledging her spirit and celebrating her time on earth while you're only dealing with her death."

He got up to pace around the room. "That's the main reason I stay here when I come to San Antonio." He pointed to the portrait. "This makes me remember and it reminds me of my anger and my regret. This is not a celebration for me, ever."

Brenna took a sip of the coffee and decided she wouldn't push him anymore right now about his sister. He was being honest with her, but he was also hinting for her to back off. "But you don't stay here a lot?"

He sat back down beside her and drank from his own cup. His expression seemed more guarded now, as if he didn't want to tell her anything else. "No. Only when I know I'll be in San Antonio for a while. My office is in town, but it's good to have this place. I'm a little too old to stay with my parents, regardless of how we're dealing with my sister's death."

"I'm too old to be living with my dad," she replied, shifting away from his family. "But I'm grateful to be home with my family for a while. My sisters and Papa have helped me through a lot of issues. Papa wants me to stay, but I'll need to decide if I'm going back to Baton Rouge one day."

"You and your family seem to handle your grief much better than my family. How's that possible?"

She put down her coffee mug and clasped her hands on her lap. "I can't explain, except that we have each other and we've always been a tight-knit family. Plus, we live in a small town where people truly love and respect each other. We had a whole community behind us when Mom died. And we have our faith."

"It always comes back to that, doesn't it?"

"For me, yes. Always." She wanted to say more, but she didn't. Nick was teaching her a new way to witness the power of Christ. She had to be patient. She had to wait. And pray.

He nibbled a chunk of cheese and a handful of grapes, more relaxed now that they weren't discussing him. "Have you considered staying in Fleur?"

Brenna didn't know the answer to that. "I honestly don't see how I can. I need a job. A long-term job." She bit into a cracker and nabbed a strawberry. "I appreciate the few months I'll be working for you, though. That'll help me through the holidays and I won't have to dip into my savings."

They sat for another minute, then he looked over at her, his expression full of hope. "Come and work for me."

Chapter Sixteen

"What?" Brenna almost dropped her mug of coffee. "Are you serious?"

"Very," he replied. "I'm always looking for qualified designers and art experts. I'd have you in one very nice package."

She tilted her head to stare over at him. "Are you offering me a job or flirting with me?"

"Both," he said through a grin.

She let that slide but fretted about their earlier conversation. "But you'd pay me twice as much, right?"

He laughed then playfully tapped her nose. "Your salary is negotiable, *sí*. And you'd be worth every penny."

Brenna got up to stare into the fire. "Me, working for you—permanently? I don't know."

"What's not to know? You love what you do and you're good at it. You've taken charge at Fleur

House, putting together rooms on spec even though the place isn't finished. You seem to know what kind of art goes in each room, what will make it perfect. That's a gift. Tia Serena is very impressed with you and you two seem to get along. You'd work mostly with her."

"I've studied art long enough to be able to gauge things like that. Nothing special. I'm not so sure—"

"Don't sell yourself short, Brenna," he said, standing to tug her close. "You're special."

Brenna finally found the courage to look up and into his eyes. She inhaled a breath when she saw the longing and need there in the richness of his dark gaze. This man confused and excited her, but he also left her wondering. "What do you really want from me, Nick?"

"This." He pulled her close and lowered his mouth to hers. "Only this."

Brenna melted into his embrace, the warmth of the fire not as sweet and toasty as the feelings brewing inside her heart. Nick's touch lifted her into a new realm of awareness.

She liked being in his arms, even if it seemed too dangerous. Even if she knew she'd be free-falling once it was over.

He stopped kissing her, then stood back. "See how well we work together?"

"Hmm. I see that I'd never get any work done

with you around. Wouldn't it be rather scandalous if a client saw me kissing the boss in every corner of a house?"

"Every corner?" He gave her a peck on the nose. "We're gonna need a bigger house."

Brenna closed her eyes and rested her head on his shoulder. She shouldn't be having so much fun in his arms. Fun kisses were one thing, but true intimacy and openness were both another. It *was* scandalous the way she seemed to be drawn to this man. That startled her, especially after she'd vowed to take her time the next time. But he had opened up to her tonight and she'd seen the horrible pain he held inside his heart.

Did she dare take on the task of soothing that pain? Working with him would be a dream, but it would also keep her in close proximity to the man. She wasn't sure she could keep that line between work and her feelings clear.

Lifting her head, she smiled up at him, hoping to hide her doubts and fears. "What is it with us? I mean, why does this feel so right?"

"You tell me," he said, his lips grazing her skin. "Sometimes people just work out together." Then he lifted his head to look into her eyes. "No matter the odds or the obstacles."

"Is that what we're doing, working out, clicking, getting along? Sharing our secrets? Have I passed another test?"

"No test," he replied, his hand touching her chin. "No test here and no secrets. This is a sure thing."

Brenna thought about Jeffrey and how she'd believed he was a sure thing. She thought about her beautiful mother who'd believed seeing her grandchildren born was a sure thing. She thought about Callie, her sweet older sister and how much Callie had tried to save her marriage while she fought against breast cancer. And she thought about Nick's little sister and wondered why Jessica hadn't lived to a ripe old age, surrounded by beautiful dark-headed grandchildren of her own.

"Nothing is for sure, Nick."

He held her chin, his gaze locking with hers. "I thought you were the one with the solid faith. Can't you have faith in us, in me?"

She wanted that. She'd prayed for that. But she'd also asked God to show Nick how to heal. Did he want to heal? Or did he want to stay in that dark place that shielded him from the world? And her? If she gave in, she might win a part of him. But Brenna wanted more. She wanted a love that gave all, that accepted the good and the bad. How would she deal with loving him if his anger simmered and festered underneath that calm exterior but never completely healed? Would he turn on her, would he forget his promises and all the odds they'd overcome?

Brenna pulled away. "I don't know. I want to believe, but you're still holding out on me."

He backed up. "In what way?"

Brenna didn't want to ask, but she had to understand. "What happened with your sister?"

He shook his head, then pointed his finger at her. "You've been talking to my aunt and my mother too much."

"No, no, I haven't," Brenna replied. "I didn't say a thing about this to your mother and your aunt won't tell me the truth out of respect for you."

Anger darkened his features. "So you've been asking around, talking to my family?"

"Of course not. I asked your aunt this morning and that was only because I saw Jessica's room."

His beautiful smile had turned into that dark scowl she'd seen before. "I shouldn't have brought you here. I tried to force this on you and now the tables are turned."

"Your family loves you," she said. "And while I don't like the shock value of what they've done, I understand the concern I saw on their faces when we got here."

"They went too far," he replied. "And so did I. I rushed things between us. It's too soon."

"It's not too soon if you trust me. I want to understand what's caused you so much pain."

"What does it matter?" he asked. "That has nothing to do with you and me and how we feel."

"I think it has everything to do with us. It's here in this house and it's back at the work site in your trailer. Your grief is stifling you, Nick. I don't know if I can bring life back to your broken heart."

"You're right. No one can do that except me. And I don't know how. It's not right of me to expect that of you, either."

Hurt that he was backpedaling after offering her what amounted to one of those stars in the sky, Brenna decided it was time to end this. She grabbed her tote bag. "I think we need to get back to town."

He let out a frustrated sigh, his gaze full of remorse now. "I'm sorry. Really."

"But not sorry enough to let me in, to show me why you can be so mercurial, so unpredictable at times. You know all about my family, my grief, my life. Why is it so hard for me to know about you?"

He turned, his hands on his hips. "You do know a lot about my life and my family, and you do know me—the real me. Why would I bring you here if I didn't trust you, Brenna?"

"I don't know." She shrugged, grabbed her wrap. "Maybe you *want* someone to force the issue. Your relatives seem to try at every turn to help you, to hope you'll be okay. Maybe you need someone with a more objective view to finally make you see the light."

"See the light? Forgive and forget? Turn back to God?" He shook his head. "I can't go that far. I can't forget. No one has to force that issue. It's just a fact, a part of my life."

"You could have a better life, Nick, if you talked to someone, tried to move past the pain I've seen in your eyes. I could help you with that. I'd *like* to help you but I don't know how. In the end, it has to be you. You have to want this."

"I am okay. I can handle this my way." He looked out the window. "And forcing me won't work. My family should realize that by now. You should realize that, too."

"I get it," she said. "I do get it, Nick. It's your business, your burden to bear. But let someone in. Let me in. Turn to God and ask Him to take away some of your pain and your guilt. I understand how you must feel, but I need to understand why you feel that way."

He whirled, anger sparking on a thread through his eyes. "You know nothing of this kind of guilt. Nothing. And I don't need your help."

No, he didn't need her to help him. He only wanted someone to help with his work, to keep him occupied and busy so he wouldn't have to think about the horror of his past, whatever that had been.

"I didn't mean to overstep," Brenna said. "I really wish you could trust someone."

"I told you, I'm okay," he said, the words ground out. "I don't know why this has to be an issue between us."

"No, you don't get it. But I do. I thought I was in love with Jeffrey, thought we'd have a life together. But he held back, never letting me in, never actually making me feel loved. Then he accused me of pushing too much or not pushing enough, you name it, I've been blamed for it. He blamed me while he partied and flirted with most of my friends and with women I didn't even know. He belittled my way of life and my family. That's not love. That's control and manipulation. I can't go through that again."

"I'm not like Jeffrey," he retorted. "I respect you, admire you. I like your way of life. I need you, Brenna."

"Yes, you need me to work with you, to keep you busy, to keep you distracted. But what happens when the sun goes down and you have me but you're still angry and bitter and suffering. What happens then, Nick?"

He stared at her, his eyes as dark as a raging river. "I'd still have you. I'd have that smile, that hope I see in your eyes. You make things better, Brenna."

Tears pricked at her eyes. "But I can't make

things right. I can't change what happened in your past. I want to, I want to make everything better, but your pain can't be my pain, Nick. I'm more than willing to listen and discuss and understand—"

"You can't understand and I can't bring myself to explain it."

She gave him one last look, then said, "We have to keep this relationship professional. Business only. I won't push you and you can't keep testing me to see if I'll get it right. That's how it has to be."

When he just stood there staring at her with that heavy torment in his eyes, Brenna pushed past him to go outside. She stared up at the inky darkness and thought he was right about one thing: the stars were much brighter out here.

And so was his pain.

They left early the next morning. Reports of the storm brewing in the Gulf were scattered all over the airwaves and the internet. What had started out as a tropical disturbance that seemed to be running its course had turned into a late-season, unpredictable tropical storm. And it was headed right for the Gulf coast. Fleur could take a direct hit unless the storm turned.

Dark clouds covered the entire coast, but it was nothing compared to the dark cloud hanging over

Brenna's head as she hugged Nick's aunt goodbye after Serena had met them for breakfast and
she'd told Serena to thank his parents for their
hospitality.

Nick sat next to her now, brooding and moody,
his nose stuck in his BlackBerry. He'd barely spoken to her after they'd had words last night. This
morning, he'd nodded to her in passing. Even
though he'd laughed and made conversation during the meal, Brenna was pretty sure his aunt had
picked up on the rift between them.

She now understood why he didn't go home
very often. He didn't want to face his family's
concern and worry. She couldn't blame him for
that, because she felt horrible about trying to force
the issue herself. But he also didn't want to face
his grief or change how it was controlling his life.
Why did grief take such a hold on people? Why
did it have to color hearts with doubt and guilt and
a deep hole of pain?

Why, Lord?

She didn't voice the prayer out loud, but she
questioned things in her heart. Why?

Why had he pushed her away?

Nick wondered that after he'd dropped Brenna
back at her car, thought about it all the way home
after she'd halfheartedly thanked him and left.
He had a million things on his mind, he thought

as he glanced at the cloudy, ominous skies, but he couldn't stop thinking about Brenna and how she made him feel. He should have known better than to take her to see his family, should have left her at the hotel while he stayed out at his house. His life was a facade and now that she'd seen that, she might not want to be around him anymore. She'd pushed him to tell her the truth but instead, he'd shoved the truth in her face with no explanations. Was he testing her again?

It sure looked that way.

But he wanted her with him, wanted her to see him with his family so she'd see that he wasn't all doom and despair. His parents grieved, yes, but they also laughed and talked and loved and they'd managed to go on with their lives. He thought he had, too. But now, after being with Brenna, he knew he'd only been sleepwalking through life. No wonder he couldn't make a commitment to a steady relationship. He was numb inside. Cold. Asleep. He needed to wake up. Really wake up.

Brenna certainly had jarred him out of his nice, safe little cocoon. Brenna made him feel alive again, forced him to face the things he'd been running from for so long. Brenna made everything beautiful. But maybe he wasn't ready to face a beautiful world, after all. Maybe he needed to punish himself for a while longer.

The time away had blown up in his face because

Brenna Blanchard wanted more. She wanted all of him. She wanted the part that he'd held away from everyone for so long now.

How could he open that cut again, bleed out in front of her while he watched the horror and disgust on her face? He couldn't do that. But it was too late, he knew. The gate to his emotions had been prodded open just enough to let her in.

Or rather, Brenna had forced her way in and refused to leave. Now he had to decide if he wanted to fight for her to stay, or fight with her until she got fed up and left.

Chapter Seventeen

The next morning, Brenna hurried with Callie around the nursery. The wind and rain had picked up overnight and Callie and her crew were checking for anything left that might go flying through the air. The forecast predicted the storm would hit sometime this afternoon or late tonight.

"The place looks great. Colorful."

Callie stopped and glanced over at her, rain hitting on their bright ponchos. "Bree, it's early November. The nursery is as drab as an old washcloth right now and a hurricane is brewing out in the Gulf, but I think it's coming faster than anyone could predict. What's the matter with you?"

Brenna snapped to and noticed the dark sky and the roaring wind. Adjusting her plastic rain poncho, she said, "I'm sorry. It's complicated."

"That is so cliché," Callie retorted, motioning for her to get under the eaves of a nearby potting shed. Holding the plastic hood of her poncho over her face, she said, "Give me something else to chew on."

Brenna shivered and held tight to her own wet poncho. "Okay, all right. It's Nick. There. Chew on that."

Elvis heard the word *chew* and came running, his woof of hopefulness endearing and annoying at the same time.

Callie patted her faithful, wet companion on the head. "Auntie Bree is in a mood today, Elvis. Don't give her a big, wet kiss."

Elvis immediately did the opposite of what his mistress had suggested. He jumped up on Brenna with two big, furry paws and tried to lick her face.

"Get off me, you ol' hound dog," Brenna said, making a face at his wet paws all over her. But she couldn't help smiling. Technically, Elvis wasn't a hound dog, but she loved using Elvis references when she was around him. "Why can't men be more like you, Elvis? All lovable and easy?"

Callie giggled. "And hairy?"

Brenna pushed the dog away and grinned. "Okay, maybe not exactly like Elvis." She took the dry towel her sister found inside the shed and handed her. "Nick doesn't like being pushed into anything. He has methods. He makes a plan and sticks to it. Apparently, that plan means he'll tell me what he wants me to know whenever he's good and ready."

"Typical male syndrome," Callie replied in a knowing tone while she scanned her domain. "What's *your* plan?"

"My plan?" Brenna squinted at her sister. "I don't have a plan. I'm going to finish the job I was hired to do and then move on."

"That is not a plan. That's a retreat."

"Yes, I'm retreating," Brenna admitted. "Look, I'm not ready for another roller-coaster ride of a relationship. I want someone who'll love me and understand me and be there for me, but I need that someone to level with me and tell me the truth. I need someone to plan a life with, to grow old with, someone I can trust always."

Callie smiled, then whistled at Elvis. The big dog came barreling up the wide aisle of palm trees and fruit trees.

"Here's your man," Callie said. "You were right. Elvis is the perfect companion. Let's get him to the shelter quick."

"Very funny."

Giving Elvis a treat for his brilliant performance, Callie turned serious. "Bree, you've always let your heart get in the way of your head. Nick seems like a perfect candidate to mend your broken heart, unless he's just gonna contribute to the already-raw wound you're carrying around."

"Oh, he's contributing all right. One minute he's kissing me and offering me a job and the next, he's pushing me away and going all stonewall on me. It's confusing."

"The old mixed-message trick," Callie said. "I never liked that one."

"What woman does? I've tried to talk to him, bring him back to God. He's bitter about his sister's death, but he won't tell me exactly what happened."

"Did you ever go back to that article you found?"

"No. I want Nick to tell me. It matters to me, his past, his hurts, his issues. Jeffrey was always so tight-lipped about things and look where that got me. If I hadn't snooped around, trying to nail him, I wouldn't have even known how much he'd tricked me and lied to me. I won't go through that again. Even if I opt for the simple plan of just working for Nick, I'd still like to know what makes him tick."

"Do you hear yourself?" Callie asked as they headed for the storefront, bending together against the driving wind. "You're trying to make Nick into what you think he needs to be. You can't force someone back to God and you can't force grief or any other problem to disappear so the world will be all better. We both should know that from first-hand experience."

Brenna stopped walking and stared over at

her sister, rain and wind hissing all around them. "You're right. I'm doing the same thing with Nick that I tried to do with Jeffrey—change him. Since we met, I've tried to force Nick at every turn. Exactly in the same way his concerned family tries to heal him and shock him into accepting what they think is best." She grabbed Callie's arm. "No wonder he doesn't want to talk to me. And, really, he's nothing like Jeffrey. Nick isn't lying about anything. He's just having a hard time with his grief, and of course, I've made that even worse. I have to go to the other plan on this."

"And what is the other plan?"

"The complicated, let's-figure-this-out plan. That one will take a lot more effort." She shrugged, glanced up at the gray, roving clouds. "Nick and I have to accept that we can weather the storms together, no matter what. He tried to tell me that, but I wouldn't listen to him. He needed me to do that. *Me.* That was his way of telling me he needed me. And what did I do? I walked away." She hit a hand against her wet hood. "I'm so dense sometimes."

Her sister stopped at the front counter inside the open nursery storefront to peel off her wet poncho. "Well, little sister, you have to decide which plan you *want* to fight for, which plan might work out best for you in the end. And going all philosophical on him might not work."

Brenna tugged at her poncho and brushed her

damp hair into place. "Honestly, I don't know if either of us is up to figuring this out, but I have to try. I have to go and talk to Nick and tell him how sorry I am."

"What if he doesn't care? What if he was trying to send you away, trying to give you an out?"

"I have to try, anyway," Brenna said. "But right now, I have to get to him before this hurricane hits."

Callie shook her head, her hand in the air. "You can't go out to Fleur House. The bridge out of town is almost under water from that tide surge that's rolling in."

"I have to go," Brenna insisted. "This can't wait. He's out there all alone. He sent everyone else to safety. It's a perfect time to tell him how sorry I am."

Her sister's usually serene face held a frown of concern. "During a hurricane? Don't you think you should wait on that?"

Brenna bit at her bottom lip. "No, what better time—he'll have to listen."

"Papa will flip out if you go into a storm, Bree."

Brenna glanced at the dark sky and the steady rain. "I have to go, Callie. I have to. Maybe I can get him to come back to town with me. We can all be together in the designated shelter."

Callie grabbed a dry bright yellow raincoat off a peg. "Take this. It's thicker than that old poncho. And be careful. Call me and let me know you made it."

Brenna nodded. After changing into the heavy raincoat, she said, "I'll call if I have service. But don't worry, I can tread water if I have to."

But once she was in her car and heading toward the curve in the Big Fleur Bayou, Brenna wondered if she'd made the right decision. The Bayou Bridge loomed ahead, old and creaky. Brenna took it slow, but she could see the angry, churning waters from the swampy river blending with the surge from the open Gulf. The water was beginning to merge over the bridge, wave by crashing wave.

Rain and wind lashed at Nick as he hurried across the yard at Fleur House. The crew had worked to secure the many windows and doors of the big house. Because they'd recently finished the major renovations inside and were now working on the outside, Nick wanted to make sure the house was secure.

Once things had been battened down, he'd sent all the workers home to be with their families, even those who'd traveled here from Texas. They could sit out the storm back in their homes instead of hotels out on the interstate.

But Nick didn't intend to leave. He had too much at stake here. He'd already reported to the owner that everything was under control. He intended to keep it that way.

His cell phone buzzed and he saw his aunt's number. Deciding to answer and reassure her before he lost cell power, he ran up on the porch to find shelter. "Hello."

"Nicky, we're all concerned about the storm. Why don't you come home?"

"You know I can't leave now, *Tia*. I have to watch over the house."

"It could be dangerous," Serena said. "That house is very close to the big water. Get somebody else to watch over it."

"This house has stood in this spot for close to two centuries and it's been through a lot of storms. I'll be fine, I promise." After promising his aunt that he'd seek cover, Nick thought of the many rooms in this big, old place. He could certainly get in the middle of the house if the wind and water got too bad. He hurried to get a weather radio, a flashlight and other supplies. He'd have those ready if he had to leave the trailer fast.

An hour later, he'd gone back over the house room by room and done everything he could to protect the huge windows and doors. Most of the windows had been shut tight with the built-in hurricane shutters he'd had installed for just such storms.

The house was dark now, the sound of the angry

wind moaning around the tree branches and flying debris hissing and hitting at the mansion. Nick was headed back to his trailer when he heard a car approaching.

Who in their right mind would be out in this coming storm?

Brenna Blanchard.

Nick had only spoken to her a few times since they'd returned from San Antonio. They couldn't work with the storm approaching, so he'd told her to stay with her father and her family and to find a safe place.

She'd obviously ignored that suggestion.

Nick turned back toward the porch and waited for her. He intended to make her turn around and go home.

Brenna, dressed in a bright yellow trench coat and rain boots, hurried up the steps onto the deep porch. "Are you all right?" she asked, out of breath.

Nick's heart took a spin at seeing her again. "Yes. What are you doing here?"

She pulled off the scarf she'd wrapped around her head. "I was worried about you. I came to bring you back to the church gymnasium. It's the designated shelter." She tugged on his arm. "But we have to hurry. The surge is covering the roads and the big bridge."

"Hold on. I have plenty of shelter right here," he

replied, pulling away. "But you need to get back to town. You can't stay here."

"I'm not going back without you," she said. "I mean it, Nick. I came to tell you I'm sorry for the way I've been acting. What can I do to help?"

Nick stared down at her, part of him wanting to tug her close while the other part of him wanted to send her on her merry way. "I think everything's under control." Except his heart. Then he looked into her eyes and said, "You don't need to apologize to me."

She stared up at him, her eyes a rich misty green-brown in the dark light. "I think I do. I've been pushing you since the day we met. Your faith and your life are none of my business. I'm so sorry."

Nick didn't know what to say. The woman had come through a storm to apologize to him when he was the one who should be explaining himself. "It's okay, Brenna. You need to go back to your family."

"I don't want to leave you out here alone. Are you sure everything is secure?"

He pointed to the windows. "We're prepared. All of the hurricane shutters are in place and all of the outside doors are shut tight. We taped over what we couldn't shutter."

"Where are you going to stay?"

He glanced toward his trailer.

Brenna followed his gaze. "No, not in there. It's too dangerous."

Nick looked up at the sky. He could tough this out. Sometimes the weather people got things wrong. "I've been through worse. I think I'll be fine. I have a weather radio. If it makes you feel better, I'll stay in the center of the house instead of my trailer."

"Have you seen the radar?" she asked, her hand motioning toward the sky. "This is a monster. It's covering the whole coast across Louisiana and Mississippi. They say it might become a Cat Three by nightfall. It's bad, Nick."

Nick checked the dark, roaring clouds, then glanced around. The rain and wind were definitely picking up. Even in a three, the surge could reach miles inland and destroy just about everything in its path. He could take care of himself, but he wouldn't be responsible for her. She should be with her family. He wouldn't risk something happening to her. He could not carry yet another burden of guilt by losing someone he loved.

Loved.

The realization tore through him with the same intensity as this storm. And because he did love her, he had to make her leave.

Tugging her toward the steps, his heart at war with his brain, he shouted, "All the more reason for you to turn around and go back to the shelter. Now, Brenna. Hurry."

Brenna watched the sky, then shook her head. Over the roar of thunder and lightning and heavy winds, she shouted, "I don't think I can go back now. The road out here was already beginning to wash out from the surge. I barely got across the bridge. I'm pretty sure it's under water by now."

As if to back her up, the heavens burst forth with heavy, heaving rain and flashing shards of thunder and lightning. Nick looked from the sky back to Brenna. He couldn't send her out in this. But what if he couldn't protect her, either?

Chapter Eighteen

"You're where?"

Brenna held her cell phone away from her ear and hit the speaker button while her papa let out a string on angry words that cleared the static coming over the wireless. "I'm with Nick at Fleur House. I don't think I can make it back to town."

"Of course you can't make it," Papa said, his words rolling together like the big waves hitting the seawall down below the house. "Da roads are washed out, de big bridge is sitting in wader. Why on earth did you think it'd be smart to go out to dat house tonight of all nights?"

Brenna could hear him even with the sound of the storm raging through the house. "I wanted Nick to come back to town with me, but he refused. I can't leave him out here all alone, Papa."

Her papa didn't agree with that decision. "Of course you can't, 'cause you're just that stubborn and impulsive, Daughter Number Three. Let me talk to da man."

"He wants to speak to you." She handed Nick her phone.

"I can hear that," Nick said to her on a whisper. "Uh, hello, Mr. Blanchard."

"Listen to me and listen good," Ramon Blanchard said. "Dat dere is my baby girl. You better take good care of her, *mon ami*. If I find one hair on her head messed up, I'll take the law into my own hands."

Nick glanced at Brenna. "Of course I'll take care of her. I told her she should have stayed in town, but I can't let her leave now."

"*Non,* she's trapped dere with you. I expect you to make sure she's safe and sound." Mr. Blanchard went on for a few more seconds, lapsing in and out of Cajun-French.

"We should be okay, Mr. Blanchard. Fleur House is built up high and the yard has a slight incline toward the bayou and swamps."

"I'm not so worried about da incline, you understand? I'm more worried about you and my daughter out dere all alone."

Nick understood what Brenna's father was telling him. "You can trust me, sir. I'll look out for her and take care of her."

"See dat you do just dat."

Nick listened, then handed the phone back to Brenna. "He's not happy and neither am I."

Brenna glared at Nick, then tried to soothe her daddy's frazzled nerves. Taking off the speaker, she said, "Papa, this is a big, old house up on a hill. I'll be as safe here as I would be in that gym."

"You just make sure dat's the case, daughter. Now go somewhere away from de wind and water. And call me back every hour on de hour until morning."

"I will unless the cell towers go out," Brenna said. "I love you."

Her father responded in kind. "I love you, too. But me, I'm thinking you love someone else better now."

A few minutes later, Brenna turned to stare at the man who'd shoved her inside the big, empty house. She watched him building a fire in the sparkling clean and updated fireplace and thought about her papa's words.

Was she in love with Nick?

She did cross a raging canal of water to get to him so she could apologize. She did want more from him, more than just a job or a friendship. She wanted to know him on an intimate, mind-to-mind, heart-to-heart level.

She was alone in a storm with a man she'd barely known a full month. And yes, she was in love with him.

But he certainly didn't look in love with her. He kept glaring at her with those dark eyes, his expression as stormy and hard to predict as the rain and wind crashing around them.

"I'm sorry," she finally said. "I should have realized you can take care of yourself, and that you didn't want me here."

Nick nodded, kept glaring. "Yes, and you should have known better than to come out in this storm. Why didn't you stay in the shelter with your family?"

"I wanted you there, too," she finally said. "I couldn't leave you out here alone, Nick."

He lifted his hands in the air, then let them drop to his side. "Why not? Why can't you leave me alone?"

Hurt by his anger, Brenna turned and stared into the big empty fireplace. Nick had lit a fire to keep them dry and warm, but the heat of his rage burned worse than the fire.

"You're right," she said, grabbing her rain slicker and heading for the front door. "I'll go. I'm sure if I hurry I can make it back across the bridge. I'd rather take a chance on that than being with you in this mood."

Then she felt his hand on her arm. "I'm sorry, too. Sorry that you felt it necessary to worry about me, necessary to come out here. Brenna, you don't need to fix me. You need someone better in your life."

He let go of her and turned away.

She whirled, her face burning in embarrassment. "Fix you? Make you better? Is that what you think I'm trying to do?" She had to close her eyes to the truth she'd already seen. She had been trying to…help him. Wasn't that the reason she'd come through that storm? To tell him she was sorry.

He stood with his arms folded and stared over at her. "Well, yes. You want me to open up to you, to tell you all about the ugliness of my life. But I can't, and I'm not the kind of man who'll ever be able to open up completely. I don't want to talk about it because it's too painful to tell."

She tugged at her resentment and swallowed her pride. "And yet, you managed to get all the details of my past out of me."

"You offered all of that," he replied, pushing off a wall to come toward the fire. Then he said on a gentle note, "You're more open and honest than I'll ever be."

"Yes, yes, I am," she retorted. "I'm honest and I expect honesty in people I care about."

That brought his head up. "You care about me?"

"Of course I do. We've been working together for weeks now. I care that you and I seem to share the same goals and we both love our work, work that seems to merge each time we're together. We complement each other. We understand each other."

"When it comes to work, you mean?"

She nodded. "But it ends there."

"And you want it to go deeper?"

"I don't know what I want," she admitted. "I don't know what I feel anymore, either." She went to the big front door and peeked through the one place he'd left open, a tiny pane of beveled glass. The yellow security light spotlighted the torrent of rain and wind. "It's getting worse out there."

"Come with me," he said, stalking toward her. "I left a weather radio in the kitchen." Then he took her hand. "And the crew set up a coffee bar in there as soon as we had power in the house. Hopefully we can find something to eat and drink before the electricity gets knocked out."

"You think it'll get really bad?" she asked, the warmth of his hand lessening the tension between them.

"Yes." He stopped and turned to her. "And even though you shouldn't have done it, I'm kinda glad I have you here with me."

Brenna took that statement and weighed it inside her heart. He tried to send her away to protect her. But he was afraid to love her. The man had to care a little bit, but she didn't know if he'd ever take things any further. And right now, she wasn't sure she even wanted that. Forcing someone to love her had never worked in her favor.

Maybe Papa was right. Had she gone off the deep end?

They made their way to the back of the house and the kitchen. "I have some candles somewhere in here," Nick said. "For ambiance. One of the locals gave me a hurricane kit."

"Good." Brenna let out a sigh of relief. "We all have a go-bag around here, filled with our most precious things and all our vital information."

Nick went to the big wide counter and found the heavy tote bag Pierre LeBlanc had brought by that morning. "Mrs. LeBlanc insisted I take this, according to Pierre. It's full of toiletries and a lot of other essentials."

"The women of the church put those together in case a hurricane comes through. Just makes things easier during and afterward."

Nick lit one of the candles and placed it on the counter. They stood silent for a while, then his eyes met Brenna's. "I'm sorry for what I said earlier. And I'm sorry our weekend ended on a bad note."

She nodded, stayed on her side of the room. "I shouldn't have forced myself on you during this storm. I really was concerned about you and I did want to apologize, too."

"You didn't force anything. I...I didn't think

I needed to leave the house. I'm responsible for this place."

"And who's responsible for your safety and well-being, Nick?"

"Only me." He shrugged. "You don't need to take on that role."

"You don't want anyone to take on that role, do you?"

"No, I guess I don't. I've learned how to take care of myself and I've been on my own for a long time."

"Since Jessica died?"

The quiet mood disappeared. His face grew as dark as the night pushing through the rain outside. "I'm not going there, Brenna."

But Brenna was going there. She didn't know why, but she figured if he couldn't talk to her about his worst pain, then they'd never be able to get along, work or no work. And even though she'd tried to apologize and so had he, they were here together and neither could leave. Maybe now *was* the best time to get it all out there.

"I almost looked it up on the internet. I saw a newspaper article and a picture of a girl on a horse—the same portrait you have over your hacienda mantel."

"Stop it."

"I never went back to finish the article. I wanted to hear it from you."

"Why? What does it matter now?"

Unsure what to say or do, she came around the corner and touched a hand to his shoulder. "Because I care, Nick. Because I've been hurt by grief. Because I worry, yes, worry about you. And pray for you."

He didn't turn around, but she felt the tension coiling inside him, felt the heat of pain and despair radiating around him. "I…can't talk about it. I don't want people to know—"

She leaned close behind him, laid her head against his broad back and wrapped her arms tight around him. "Why? Because it will hurt? Because you're afraid I'll turn away? This is me, Nick. I don't do that. I don't turn away. I turn toward the things I want in life."

Then she heard a low, growling whisper. "Do you want me, then, in your life?"

"Yes, yes, I think I do. But I want all of you, not just the parts you want me to see." She held on to him. "I'm sorry, but I have to be honest. And I need you to be honest."

"You might not like what you see if I show you everything."

"Let me be the judge of that," she said. "Please, Nick?"

He turned then, his eyes a deep, dark pool of anger and grief. "I don't think—"

A crash outside brought them apart. Nick took

her by the hand and tugged her upstairs. "There's a port window on the staircase. I left it uncovered but it's got tape across it. Maybe we can see out that."

Startled and disoriented, Brenna followed him and waited while he squinted into the dark night. "The security lights are still on." He turned back to her, his features a mixture of concern and regret. "But the seawall didn't hold back the surge. It looks like the whole front yard is flooded with water."

They lost electricity around midnight.

Brenna sat huddled with Nick in the upstairs sitting room. He'd assured her the floodwaters shouldn't reach them up here.

Now, she prayed the water wouldn't damage the bottom floor. But this was only a house. She also prayed that everyone she loved would be safe. All they could do was wait and watch. And continue to pray.

"I'm glad I called Callie earlier," she said. "They'd all be so worried. And they don't need to know about the seawall breaking."

Nick sat with his hands resting on his knees. "If the water has reached that high, I'm pretty sure they've seen it in town, too. It's gonna be a long night."

Brenna saw the shadows moving across his

face. The candlelight traced his fatigue. "I guess I should have stayed in town. Now you feel responsible for me, too."

He shook his head. "I didn't mean— I wasn't talking about your being here. This storm could rage for hours." He touched a finger to her still-damp curls. "It's as stubborn as you, I think."

"You're comparing me to a hurricane?"

"You do tend to push through walls and come crashing onto a scene."

She didn't respond to that because she knew it was true. "I don't always think things through."

He tugged at the strands he had around his finger. "And I don't always say what I really mean."

The house rattled. They heard more crashing sounds.

"Why don't we go check on the bottom floor?" she asked. "I promise I won't do anything crazy. I'll be right behind you."

He'd refused this idea earlier, telling her he couldn't risk her getting injured. Now he stared over at her with those dark eyes. "You amaze me."

Shocked, she drew her head back. "What? Me? Why?"

"You have this positive attitude, even in the middle of a hurricane. For every doubt I throw out there, you have a reassurance. It's one of the things I—admire about you."

Her heart hammered in a heavy cadence, so she

tried to keep her words light. "Oh, there's more than one thing you admire about me?"

He leaned close. "Yes, lots more."

She swallowed, her throat going dry. "Then tell me."

He shifted, then touched her hair again. "I admire your hair." He pushed his fingers through her tangled locks.

"It's frizzing right now," she said, her heart doing that excited beat.

"You look good in frizzy hair."

She grinned at that. "Thank you."

He moved a little closer. "And I love those big ever-changing eyes." Then he held up her chin so he could feather her nose with kisses. "And I like this. Being with you like this, in spite of all the things that brought us here together in this storm, means the world to me."

Brenna drew back to stare up at him. "Nick, I need you to understand something."

He pressed a kiss to her temple. "But I'm not through admiring all your good qualities."

She put her hand on his face. "I don't have such good qualities. I've been pushy, nosy, demanding. When I go after something or someone, I *do* want it all. It's the way God wired me, but I'm trying to change. I think that's why Jeffrey and I didn't work."

Nick grabbed her hand in his. "Jeffrey was an idiot to treat you so badly and to let you get away."

"Or maybe he was smart to end things before he got trapped in a marriage with me."

"You can't be serious?"

"I am very serious. I'm seriously flawed. The whole time I've known you, I've badgered you about your past when really, all that matters is the future."

"Our future, you mean?"

"Do you want a future with someone like me in it?"

"No," he said, his expression solemn and unyielding.

Brenna's heart sank like a battered boat. "Well, then—"

"I don't want someone *like* you. I want *you* in my future."

A new shock wave flowed through her. "Working with you?"

He smiled, then kissed her hand. "That and more."

Brenna didn't know what to say. But Nick didn't give her time to speak. He tugged her into his arms and kissed her.

Brenna fell into that kiss with a feeling of falling into that raging water down below them. A floating sensation took over and purged all of her doubts and fears. She didn't need to know the truth about Nick's tragic past. She only knew one truth right now.

She loved him.

Nick lifted his head and hugged her. "Everything is going to work out for us, Brenna."

"What makes you so sure of that?"

"I have faith," he said, his smile soft and sure. "Because of you, I have faith in us."

She blinked at the tears pricking at her eyes. "I guess that's one of my positive attributes, huh?"

"*Sí*. The best one next to your sweet lips."

She couldn't speak, didn't understand the full meaning of his calm words. What had changed inside that fascinating mind? When he stood and reached down for her, she almost didn't get up. She wasn't sure she would be steady on her feet.

"Let's go check the water," he said. "If everything looks okay, we'll sit down and have a long talk."

"About us?" she had to ask. "About our future?"

He stopped on the landing. "No, about me. About my past."

Chapter Nineteen

Nick found a flashlight and guided Brenna down the stairs. Shining the wide beam ahead of them, he could hear the never-ending roar of the wind and water whirling with gale strength around the big house. The weather radio warning indicated the storm had made landfall dead-center between Louisiana and Mississippi. Things could have been much worse, but there would be millions of dollars of damage all the same.

"Steady," he said as he stayed in front of her. "Be careful."

"I'm right here," Brenna replied, her hand holding tight to his shirt.

Nick thought that certainly was an appropriate statement. Brenna had been right here from the beginning. She'd come home for her sister's wedding even when her own heart was breaking because she'd just called off things with her fiancé.

Nick had danced with her at that wedding because he wanted to get to know her. The attraction was there even in those first awkward moments. He couldn't deny that. He'd offered her a job because of her expertise and experience, but he'd wanted her near so he could enjoy being around her.

And he realized now, as he thought about the mural she'd begged him to restore, that Brenna was a lot like that big, oversize depiction of a long-ago way of life. She was a bit tattered and torn, but she was larger-than-life and she held a deep beauty that couldn't be denied. He'd fallen for her that day when she'd stared up at that mural, probably had fallen for her when he'd look up and saw her at the wedding.

He'd tried to deny that, but he'd at least been honest when he'd told her what he wanted more than anything. "Make it beautiful for me."

She could do that and more. She could make his life new and fresh and full of hope and love instead of doubt and grief and regret.

But first, he had to be completely honest with her.

Brenna demanded that above all else.

And he would tell her everything, as soon as he knew she'd be safe in this house. They made it to the landing above the first floor. The whole house seemed to be shaking and shimmying against the power of that wind. But from what he could tell from the long beam of light, the bottom floor was intact.

"No water down here so far," he said, glad for the distraction. "I'll need to check the basement."

"The basement!" She held even tighter to him. "You can't go down there. It's dark and spooky and if water is coming in, you might bump into snakes and alligators."

"I don't think they can make it through the new mesh screens we installed on the windows."

"You never know."

But he did know a lot of things now that he'd never known before. Brenna kept pushing, pushing until he had to take a long hard look at himself and his own shaky faith.

Why did it have to take a storm to get him to stop and take a long, hard look at his life? And to realize he was truly in love for the first time, the last time if he had his way.

"Let's check the port window," he said, glancing behind him. He held the light up toward the round little window, but it was hard to see in the darkness. "I can't tell with the rain and wind blowing so hard. It's dark out there with no security lights."

"Let's keep going," she said, her hand on his arm.

When they reached the bottom floor, he turned to stare up at her. "Are you okay?"

"I'm fine," she said. "Just glad I'm here with you."

"What about your family?"

"They know I'll be all right."

"You trust me that much?"

She let out a breath. "Yes, I do."

"I don't deserve your trust."

"And I don't deserve you."

He helped her down the last stairstep, thinking she might change that assumption. The windows rattled and shook while the wind hit at the house like a construction worker with a sledgehammer. Nick heard debris pelting against the porches and the windows and wondered if anything would be left of the yard. Thankfully, he'd had his foreman move all the heavy machinery and tools to a safer location.

"Where's your car?" Brenna asked.

"Julien let me put it in his boat shop."

"That's good. I love that car."

Nick had to smile at her nervous chatter. He loved that car, too. "The car should be okay. Julien seems to have some experience with storms."

"Oh, yes. His brother and my papa got lost in one last spring, in a boat that Julien built."

"I've heard about that. They survived. We will, too."

She grabbed at him when they entered the big, empty dining room. "What if Fleur House doesn't survive?"

Once, just a few short weeks ago, Nick would

have been devastated by that kind of talk. It would have painted him as a failure. Now, he looked around, shining the flashlight's beam here and there.

And he only saw one thing that mattered.

Brenna.

"I'm not worried about that. I only want you to survive."

She looked up at him, her eyes shining bright in the faint glow the flashlight provided. "I'm tough. It'll take more than a hurricane to sweep me off my feet."

Nick decided he wanted to be the one to sweep her away. He was tired of fighting his feelings, tired of carrying his heavy burden, so tired of living in the shadow of his guilt and shame. He might not deserve any happiness, but he couldn't fight this any longer. He needed Brenna in his life.

"Hold tight," he said, pulling her with him. "I'll need your help when we reach the basement door."

Brenna wasn't so sure about this. She'd never really liked basements. But then, she'd never really gone in a lot of basements, either. But Nick was with her and that did bring her a measure of security and calm.

The irony of their situation hit at her with the same force as the wind and rain pelting the house.

Nick was going to open up to her so they could have a future together.

Maybe getting dirty in a dank basement was a metaphor for their relationship. They had to get into the thick of things to make it through. She'd certainly pushed him, fought with him, forced him to confront whatever he seemed to be holding him back.

And what about you? she asked herself. Hadn't she been holding back in her own life? She'd practically run away from Fleur to put the tragedy of her mother's death behind her. Then Callie had gotten sick and Brenna had poured herself into work and trying to please Jeffrey because she didn't want to face the fear of a dreaded disease. Callie was more upbeat and positive than any of them, and yet, Brenna had shied away from telling her brave, remarkable sister how proud she was of her.

And now, she'd found a man who could deal with her quirks and her fears, but he was afraid to confront his own shortcomings and guilt. Would she run from him, too?

They were at the basement door now.

Nick turned to her. "Are you ready?"

"I think so." She kissed him for good measure.

He listened through the massive door right off the new kitchen. "The workers haven't done much down here, but it's pretty sturdy. It's held up this house for a long, long time."

Brenna bobbed her head. Nick turned the doorknob and slowly pushed it open, then he shined the light down the stairs.

Brenna glanced over his shoulder. She heard it before they saw it. "Water."

"It's three steps away," Nick said. "Any higher and the bottom floor will be flooded."

"What can we do?"

"Hope the storm passes quickly so this can start receding," he replied.

"What about sandbags, a way to seal off the rest of the house?"

He shook his head. "We counted on the seawall to hold, so we put down only a few sandbags around the base of the house and obviously those didn't hold, either."

Brenna wasn't afraid for herself. They could go to the top of the house if they had to. But she hated to see this great old house go through a flood so soon after being renovated.

"Is this the only door to the basement?"

He nodded. "If the surge begins to recede, we'll be okay."

"This means the surge did reach the house," Brenna said. "I don't know if that's ever happened before."

"We'll rebuild the seawall," he replied as they turned toward the kitchen. "We'll make it stronger."

Brenna smiled in spite of her fears. Nick was in this for the long haul. Maybe he'd use that same declaration regarding their relationship, too.

They reached the kitchen and he motioned to two plastic chairs the construction guys had left behind. "Nothing we can do now but wait. Let's sit a minute. I'll check the water level again in a bit."

He offered her a banana he found on the counter. "You must be starving."

"I'm okay."

Brenna kept thinking about upstairs and how he'd reached for her, how he'd kissed her and told her he wanted her in his future. Had he only said those things because he was trapped here with her? Because this storm made him think of what could or could not happen?

They sat in silence for a few minutes while she finished her banana. The wind continued its assault against the house, the rain drowning out the rest of the world. Her phone didn't have any reception, but she wondered how Papa and Callie and the rest of her family and friends were faring. The water was so close, so very close.

Nick got up. "I'll check again."

Brenna closed her eyes and said a prayer for all the people she loved. Suddenly, she wanted her family near, wished she could have convinced Nick to go back to town with her.

But God had put her here for a reason, storm or no storm.

She didn't have it in her to abandon Nick, the same as when that other storm had hit and her papa and Pierre had gone missing. She'd driven through that storm to get home.

She'd driven through this storm to find her heart.

"Brenna?"

She opened her eyes to find Nick standing over her.

"What?"

"I don't think the water's getting any higher. The surge probably pushed through the garden and grounds and met up with the bayou on the low end of the property. We'll have to keep watch, but if that rain settles down, I think maybe we'll be okay."

She nodded, tears pushing at her tired eyes.

He motioned to the dining room. "Let's go look at the mural."

Thinking this was an odd time for that, she got up, anyway.

Nick took her into the big, empty room, then pulled her close. "Let's dance."

"We don't have music."

"We don't need music."

He started humming a soft, sweet tune and she fell into his arms. "This is nice."

He kissed her near her temple. "The storm is out there, but we're okay in here."

She laid her head on his shoulder and closed her eyes. "Yes, we're okay."

They danced for a few minutes, then he stopped and looked down at her. "I...I blame myself for what happened to Jessica."

"I know," she said, her heart hurting for him.

"Is it that obvious?"

"Sometimes you look like you have the weight of the world on your shoulders."

"It feels that way at times."

She waited, patient now because she knew how much this had cost him.

He pulled her close again. "We still lived out on the ranch. Not in the hacienda, but in our house a few miles away. She was taking horseback riding lessons. She knew how to ride a horse, but this was for a competition, not a rodeo. But more formal."

"Dressage?"

"Yes. I was angry because she needed a ride to the stables where she was trained and Mom and Dad had gone into town to take care of some banking business. They expected me to take her to her lesson and they'd planned to meet her there later. Her horse was already there. We boarded him there away from the other animals. I had a date that night and I was in a mood, rushing her around, calling her names. I didn't want to give her a ride and when she finally got in the truck, she was pouting because her big brother had shouted at her."

Brenna closed her eyes, an image forming inside her head. But she didn't dare ask what had happened.

"She was late because of me. I was going through this phase where I resented everything my parents tried to do for us. It seemed they were spoiling Jessica. I told her that. She didn't want to get in trouble with her instructor, though, so she got in and just sat there, tears in her eyes." He paused, took a breath.

Brenna could hear the wind howling, pushing, fighting at the house. The rain hit harder and harder against the windows.

She held tight to the man in her arms, willing him to talk to her.

"I had planned to drop her off and leave, but she turned to me with those big brown eyes. 'Nicky, won't you stay and watch?'"

He stopped, stood back to slide his hand down his face. "She was fifteen, Brenna. Fifteen. I was eighteen and hotheaded, determined to get back at her for bothering me. I was selfish and in a hurry to get to my girl. I laughed and told her I didn't have time to sit around watching her on some stupid horse."

He walked to the mural and stared into the darkness. "The funny thing is I'd painted a portrait of her on that very horse about a month before that. We wanted to give it to our parents for their anniversary."

Brenna put a hand to her mouth to stop the gasp of anguish.

"The picture hanging on your wall, the same one I saw on the internet?"

He nodded. "The local paper did a story on her, on her death, and my mother showed them the portrait. So tragic, such a waste of a young girl's dreams."

Brenna rushed to him. "Nick, don't. Don't say anything else."

But he was ready to talk now. "No, you need to understand. You need to see what kind of person I was then. I was selfish and I wanted more—I wanted the big city and money and I wanted to design great houses and buildings, but I was stuck on this ranch, working day and night and trying to finish school. We had to sacrifice to buy that horse for her. Always for her."

"Nick—"

He held up a hand. "I only painted the portrait because she wanted to surprise our parents, wanted to thank them for believing in her. So I

painted her, hoping they'd be proud of me, too."
He shook his head. "They were always proud of
me, but I was too blind to see that."

He paced back and forth, then turned to face
Brenna. "I walked back to my truck and I got
inside even while she stood there crying." He
stopped, put a hand to his face. "I left her there
and peeled out, spewing rocks everywhere. The
old truck backfired. It was so loud."

When he gulped a breath, Brenna grabbed at
his hand and held it.

"All that noise spooked one of the horses and it
came charging around the corner and… She was
standing there, waving to me, but it kept coming
and the horse reared back and kicked and kicked
and—"

Brenna pulled him into her arms, held him
while his body shuddered. "The horse kicked
her in the head and kept running. I was at the
end of the drive. I turned to look back, thinking
I shouldn't leave her that way. I glanced over, de-
bating whether to go back or not, and I saw the
horse charging toward her, saw her trying to protect herself. I called out, then I got out of the truck
and ran toward her, but it was too late, too late."

He held on to Brenna. "She died instantly, according to the doctors." He sniffed and stood back
to wipe his eyes. "My mother found the portrait a
week later in Jessica's closet."

He finally looked at Brenna. "I stopped painting after that. I didn't want to live after that. But I did live. My heart kept right on beating, so I finished college and I worked and worked, but I couldn't keep the memory of that day out of my mind. I build beautiful homes for families, for people to live in and play in and laugh in, but I didn't think I deserved such things. My parents kept telling me it wasn't my fault, but I knew it was. It was, Brenna. I caused my little sister's death."

"No," she said, trying to reach out to him. "No, Nick. You turned. You were going back."

"She never knew that. She was crying and then she tried to shield herself. I see that image every day, every night, and I have to live with that the rest of my life."

Brenna swiped at the tears streaming down her face. "So you live in a trailer to punish yourself?"

"No, I live in a trailer so I can keep moving."

"But you can't get away from this grief."

"No. And I can't get away from asking God why? Why Jessica? Why wasn't it me that day? Why am I still here when she's gone forever?"

Brenna grabbed for him, her fingers willing him to relax. "You're a good man, Nick. I can see that. Your family loves you. God loves you. I love you, too. And you will see Jessica again one day."

He shook his head, pulled away. "No. I was so angry at God for so long. I buried all that anger and pain in my work. But then, you came along and shattered everything I'd built around my heart. I wanted to get out of here and keep going. I didn't want to face you or God." He looked down at her, his heart in the dark torment of his eyes. "But now, I want you both in my life."

She reached for his hands and held them tight, her eyes searching his, tears falling down her face. "We're here. I'm here and God never turned from you. It's okay, you can rest now." She pulled him into her arms, her hand massaging his back. "You can stop running now, Nick."

Chapter Twenty

Nick woke with a start.

He was sitting against a wall in the second-floor hallway with Brenna in his arms, her raincoat covering her. She sighed and opened her eyes to look up at him.

"I don't hear rain," she said. She sat up and pushed at the coat. "Nick, I think it's over."

"It's morning," he said. "Early yet." He checked his watch. "Six-fifteen. It's still drizzling, but we should be okay now."

"I have to call Callie and Alma."

She lifted up before he could move to help her.

While she paced and waited to hear, Nick thought over the long night. Brenna loved him. She'd told him that.

She wanted him to stop running from his guilt. Could he do that? He'd never actually talked to anyone other than his family about that day and

what had happened to Jessica. They kept telling him they didn't blame him, but in his heart he'd always felt that they did. His parents loved him, but how could they ever forgive him? How could he forgive himself?

He'd told Brenna everything, the whole ugly story.

And she hadn't turned away. She'd held him and comforted him and he knew she'd prayed for him. Did he deserve her? Did he deserve her understanding? Did he deserve God's love and forgiveness?

He kept remembering what she'd said once. She turned toward the things she wanted. Nick realized she was right. He ran from the things he really wanted—a home, a family, a faith-based life—because he didn't think he deserved those things. And with Brenna, he'd worried that if he loved her too much, God would somehow punish him by taking her away. What if she got breast cancer? Could he handle that now?

Brenna thought he was worth fighting for, and she believed that Christ thought he was worth fighting for. Could he really have the kind of life he'd only dreamed about?

Nick got up to see if he could get through to his parents. His phone signal was weak, but he could hear the phone ringing.

"Hello?"

"Mama, it's Nick. I'm okay. I haven't checked outside the house yet, but I think we made it."

"Oh, Nicky, I'm so thankful. I asked so many people to pray for all of you."

"Thanks, Mama." He glanced at Brenna. She was talking, her hands moving in animation. Her hair was down and falling all around her face, her shirt and jeans rumbled, her feet bare. She'd never looked more beautiful.

Nick talked to his mother a little longer. "I'd better go, but before I do, I need to tell you something."

"What is it?" his mother asked. "Are you sure you're okay?"

"I told Brenna about Jessica, Mama. I told her about that day and what really happened."

"Nicky." His mother lapsed into Spanish. She thanked God and everyone else she could think of. "I'm so glad. Brenna, she understands. She cares for you because she has the love of Christ in her heart. She is a good girl, *sí?*"

"*Sí,*" he replied. "She's special."

His mother's next words were shaky. "Nicky, we love you so much. All is forgiven. All, Nicky. It's time for you to forgive yourself."

"I think maybe you're right," he said. "It's so hard, but I'm trying. Brenna has helped me a lot with that."

He hung up and turned to stare at the woman at the other end of the long, dark hallway. Brenna put her phone away and came toward him. "They're all okay. They have some damage and leakage in the church gymnasium, the roads are still flooded and a few buildings and homes are damaged. But it's not nearly as bad as it could have been. Callie said they were getting reports of other areas that got the brunt of it. We'll need to help out there."

Nick didn't say anything. He just pulled her into his arms and held her. He wanted to say so many things. He wanted to tell her that he loved her, that he'd fallen for her the first time he'd seen her. But these feelings rushing through him were every bit as powerful as the storm that had bombarded them through the night. They'd been spared the worst of the hurricane, and he'd been spared the pain and agony of his guilt.

"Are you all right?" Brenna asked, lifting away to stare up at him.

"I'm good," he replied. "I feel lighter, less burdened."

"Confession is good for the soul," she replied. Then she took his hand in hers. "Nick, it wasn't your fault."

"It will always be my fault," he said. "My anger and refusal to stay, the truck backfiring, the skittish horse breaking loose—it all happened because of me. I know I can't change any of it, but Jessica would want me to be happy. She'd tell me I'm being silly, that I can't control the world."

"I wish I could have known her," Brenna replied.

"I do, too. She would have loved you." He kissed her, then looked her in the eye. "I love you."

Brenna's eyes filled with tears. "I love you, too." She smiled up at him. "We probably need to check on things."

"Yes. Let me get the radio and see what's being reported."

The new wasn't good. The worst of the storm had gone east of Fleur, but the spin-off had done enough damage to bring everything to a halt. Roads and homes were under water and several businesses had sustained considerable damage.

"We'd better stay here awhile longer," he said. "The bridge back to town might not be safe."

Brenna agreed. "I don't even know if my car is still around. But we don't have to worry. Someone will come and get us by boat if they have to."

"Probably your father," Nick replied, his thoughts somber. "And I can't say that I blame him."

"Papa knows he can trust me. And I think he must trust you, too. If not, he would have come through that storm to fetch me home."

He laughed at that. "I have this image—"

"I'm serious. My papa means business."

"I believe you. But he *can* trust me. *You* can trust me."

Brenna had felt a bit awkward in the light of day, after hearing the tragic story of Jessica's death. But now, she turned to Nick and put her arms around him. "And now, you know you can trust me." She stood back to stare up at him. "It must have been awful, carrying around all that guilt for so long. I hope now you can begin to heal."

Nick pulled her close. "Yes, I think so." He kissed her on the nose. "There is so much I want to say to you. But right now, I need to check outside."

After eating granola bars and washing them down with tepid water, Brenna and Nick opened the front door to survey the grounds.

"Well, I'll definitely need Callie's help in restoring the gardens," he said.

The front yard was still standing in about a foot of water. Brenna could tell where the water had come and gone because some of the bushes and young saplings were bent and still leaning almost to the ground. The force of the water and wind had caused everything to shift, and in some places, trees and limbs lay broken.

Brenna moved from one side of the big porch

to the other, looking for her car. She let out a gasp and forgot about that for now. "Nick, your trailer is gone."

Nick rushed down the steps to stand in the muddy water. "Unbelievable." He pointed out toward the back of the property where a small bayou was now overflowing and full of debris.

"It's sitting in the water in the middle of the little bayou. And your car is jammed up against it."

Brenna came down the steps. "The water carried the trailer and my car right into the stream."

He nodded. "That's probably what caused the crash we heard last night. That cypress stopped both from floating away."

"Did you have anything valuable in the trailer?"

He turned to look at her and her breath stopped. "Not as valuable as you," he said, his eyes moving over her face.

"I'm serious, Nick."

"So am I."

He took her hand. "I have my laptop and my files and blueprints inside the house, but honestly, right now I don't care about that. I'm just glad you're okay and that no one we know died in this storm."

"I feel the same." She glanced around. "But your trailer is totaled."

Nick put his hand on her face. "Brenna, I don't need that trailer anymore."

Brenna's heart hit at her rib cage. "You don't?"

He shook his head. "No." Then he brought her close. "I think I've found my home. It's wherever you are."

"Nick," she said on a soft sigh. "Nick."

He kissed her, then lifted her up and carried her back to the porch. Brenna didn't protest. Being in his arms felt right, no matter the circumstances.

When he set her down, she stared up at him. "Are you sure? I know how much you loved that trailer."

"No, you're wrong on that."

Surprised, she said, "But—"

"I never said I loved it," he interjected. "I thought I needed to live there. But Brenna, I needed so much more. I wanted so much more."

She nodded in understanding. "Just like me. I've always wanted more." Then she smiled. "But right now, I think I have exactly enough."

Then they heard a sound off in the distance. Brenna listened and waited as the low roar got closer. Through the trees, she spotted a boat with two men aboard slowly making its way through the murky flood waters.

Nick squinted through the muted sunlight. "I think the cavalry has arrived."

Brenna smiled. "It's Papa and Julien."

"Do they have guns?" Nick asked, grinning.

"Of course not." She waved at them. "Well, they

might. You know there are all sorts of predators in these waters."

"You have a point," Nick replied.

Brenna waved. "Papa, we're here."

Her papa waved as Julien pulled up the motor and maneuvered the trolling boat up into the yard with paddles. "Dere's Daughter Number Three."

Julien grinned and called out. *"Bonjour!"*

Brenna couldn't hide the tears misting her eyes. Nick took her hand and squeezed it. "You're safe now."

But Brenna knew she'd found her heart. She'd always be safe with Nick. And she'd make sure she safeguarded his heart by showing him how much she loved him.

After greeting her father and her brother-in-law and assuring Papa that she was okay, Brenna gathered the things she and Nick needed while the men went down to survey the basement.

"It's still underwater," Nick told her when they came back up. "We'll have to pump it out, but I think the basement is still sound. We'll have to figure out what happens next, but I'll worry about that. We need to get you back to town."

"You're coming, too, right?"

"Course he is," Papa said, his gaze on Nick. "We'll need his help. Lots of things need our attention."

Nick readily agreed and soon they were on their

way back up what used to be the main road into town. Along the way, Julien pointed out some of the worst of the damage.

"Papa, what about our house?" Brenna asked.

"Da carport is gone," Papa said with a shrug. "And the back porch is damaged. But we can fix dat. Again." He let out a little chuckle. "At least dis time, I know me some good decorators and architects." He winked at Nick. "Tell your aunt we'll be giving her some business real soon."

Nick laughed at that. "She'll be happy to help."

Brenna glanced from her papa to the man she loved.

As the sun rose pink and fresh over the flooded bayou, she lifted her head and thanked God for this beautiful day. And for the man who'd come into her life broken and burdened.

They could finish Fleur House together. Because they'd both been through their own restoration. And she knew even though there would be other storms and other challenges, God was still working on her and Nick. With His grace, they'd survive.

Epilogue

Two weeks later

Nick looked around the long table and smiled. Thanksgiving at the Blanchard house was different from any other Thanksgiving he'd ever attended. Different and so much better.

Brenna sat beside him, while Julien and Alma were next to her. Callie sat across from them, then his Tia Serena and his parents were on the other side of the table, along with Pierre and Molly and Mrs. LeBlanc. Papa Blanchard sat at the head, grinning big.

"Dis is the best Thanksgiving we've had in a month of Sundays," Mr. Blanchard declared. He glanced up at the picture of his deceased wife. "Lila, we know you're up dere pulling some strings for us, belle." He stopped, cleared his throat. "And we know you got a whole passel of angels with you." He glanced at Nick, then looked around the table. "We are a blessed bunch, *oui?*"

A chorus of *oui* and *sí* followed.

"Den let's eat us some turkey and dressing."

Callie nodded. "But first, we bless the food."

Elvis put his nose to the back door and barked.

After Mr. Blanchard said grace, the meal progressed. Nick had never seen so many side dishes or desserts. Two very distinctive cultures had come together for this meal, so no one would go hungry.

He glanced over at Brenna. "I'd like to talk to you after we eat. In private."

"Really? What's the big secret?"

He shrugged. "No secret. I just haven't had a minute alone with your since the storm."

"We have been busy," she said. "Okay, I'll meet you out back under the arbor after dessert."

Nick dived into the meal and thought about the last two weeks. They'd all been clearing, cleaning and rebuilding. His family had come earlier in the week to help out. Fleur House was back on track, but he'd offered to lend out several of his construction workers to help with other needs. His boss had been very generous in anonymously giving a huge donation to the town of Fleur. The money had been put to good use and they'd all worked hard to fix what needed fixing. He couldn't believe he could be so happy. He couldn't believe he'd finally found a real home.

So after the big meal, while everyone sat back and groaned at being so full, he walked outside and waited for Brenna underneath the white arbor. It was a crisp fall day, but the temperatures were pleasant and the sun was bright. Two squirrels fussed in the moss-covered oak that shaded most of the backyard.

He watched them until he heard a door open and shut.

Brenna came hurrying toward him, her long skirt swishing against her suede boots. "I'm here. What's the big deal?"

Nick pulled her into his arms. "You," he said. "You are a very big deal."

She grinned and slapped him on the chest. "I think you just wanted to be alone with me."

"I did."

"Me, too," she said. "I've missed this."

Nick had missed their alone time, too. "I think I have a way to remedy this situation," he said, his heart jumping and skipping.

She drew back, her eyes almost golden in the sunlight. "What's that?"

He pulled a black box out of his pocket, then got down on one knee. "*Te amo.* I love you."

Brenna let out a gasp, her hand going to her heart. "Nick?"

Nick looked at her beautiful face. "Brenna, you are my home, *mi corazón.*" He opened the box and took out the ring.

"Nick?"

He heard the joy in her voice, saw that same joy in her eyes. It reflected exactly how he felt.

He took her hand and said, "Will you marry me?"

Brenna gasped again, then sank down on her knees and hugged him close. "Yes, of course. I love you so much."

Nick breathed a sigh of relief and placed the antique ring on her finger. "This was my grandmother's ring. My mother gave it to me when I told her I wanted to marry you. If you don't—"

"It's perfect," Brenna said. "Just perfect."

Nick kissed her. "I'm not perfect—just remember that."

"You are to me," she said.

He held her close, savoring the new joy that flowed like pure water through his soul. "Remember that day I told you to make it beautiful for me?"

"The mural, you mean? Yes, I remember."

He looked into her eyes and finally told her his last secret. "I wasn't talking about the mural."

"I know," she said with a smile. "How am I doing?"

"You make everything beautiful."

He kissed her again, then stood and helped her up.

They stayed that way for a few minutes, then turned to go inside and announce their good news.

But they didn't have to do that. Callie came running out, screaming and laughing and crying. "Let me see this ring I've been hearing about."

"You knew?" Brenna asked, wiping away tears. Alma was right behind her, tears on her face.

Callie hugged her sister close, her gaze on Nick. "Of course we knew about the ring, but *I* knew from the beginning."

Nick smiled. "*Sí,* your sister is very wise."

"Yes, I am," Callie said, giving him a hug, too.

Then the whole family spilled out into the yard, everyone laughing and crying and speaking in two different languages.

But Nick understood now. Restoration was good for the soul.

He looked up toward the trees and saw a golden-green butterfly fluttering through the air. And he could have sworn he felt the touch of an angel's wings caressing his face.

* * * * *

Dear Reader,

I hope you enjoyed this second story in my Cajun series. Brenna is a lot like me, I think (drama queen!). But she learned to reel in on overreacting to things. This helped her when it came to waiting for Nick to open up to her. She wanted to rush things along, but she also learned that sometimes things have to happen in God's own time.

Nick held back his emotions and his doubts because he thought he was unworthy in God's eyes. He couldn't share his deepest pain with anyone, but Brenna did bring him to a spot where he realized he had to let go of the past and his guilt.

These two opposite personalities came together through God's grace and a yearning inside both of them. I think we all yearn for something that we know is just out of our reach. But Christ is right there with us, lifting us up on our faith journey.

Soon comes Callie's happily ever after. I hope you'll bear with me until it's finished. She will meet the mysterious owner of Fleur House and change his life forever!

Until next time, may the angels watch over you—always.

Lenora Worth

Questions for Discussion

1. Why did Brenna return to Fleur? Do you think children who move away should come home after going through a life change?

2. What is the bond that holds Brenna and her sisters together? Have you ever shared such a bond with someone?

3. Why does Brenna need to know about Nick's past? Why is it so hard for her to trust in God and in Nick?

4. Brenna is a bit impulsive and dramatic. Do you know someone who acts and reacts in this way? Is it hard to deal with this type of personality?

5. Nick held a tragic secret in his heart and blamed himself. Have you ever blamed yourself for something that happened in your past?

6. Why did Nick refuse to talk about this tragedy? Do you think men have a harder time dealing with grief?

7. Nick restores homes, but he can't restore his

own heart. Why do you think he cared about restoring houses so much?

8. The overall theme of this book is restoration. Christ can bring restoration to our hearts. Why is this so important to Brenna?

9. Nick's family tried to put on a good front, but their grief still shined through. Have you ever known someone who dealt with grief in a way that seemed different? How did you handle this?

10. Nick loved art and so did Brenna. What is it about art, especially portraits of people, that brings out strong emotions?

11. Brenna realized Nick held a deep hurt in his heart. Do you think she handled this in the right way? What could she have done differently?

12. Time and circumstance can help a grieving person to heal, but Nick didn't want to let go of his grief. How did he finally see that he needed to do this?

13. Do you think meeting Brenna helped Nick to finally heal? How did her strong faith help Nick?

14. Brenna's family ties were strong, even though she'd been through tragedy, too. Nick's family had a strong bond, but they were still in denial. How were the two families the same? How were they different?

15. Do you believe Nick and Brenna are a good match? Do you believe God plays a role in bringing two people together?

REQUEST YOUR FREE BOOKS!

2 FREE INSPIRATIONAL NOVELS
PLUS 2
FREE
MYSTERY GIFTS

Love Inspired

YES! Please send me 2 FREE Love Inspired® novels and my 2 FREE mystery gifts (gifts are worth about $10). After receiving them, if I don't wish to receive any more books, I can return the shipping statement marked "cancel." If I don't cancel, I will receive 6 brand-new novels every month and be billed just $4.49 per book in the U.S. or $4.99 per book in Canada. That's a savings of at least 22% off the cover price. It's quite a bargain! Shipping and handling is just 50¢ per book in the U.S. and 75¢ per book in Canada.* I understand that accepting the 2 free books and gifts places me under no obligation to buy anything. I can always return a shipment and cancel at any time. Even if I never buy another book, the two free books and gifts are mine to keep forever.

105/305 IDN FVYV

Name	(PLEASE PRINT)

Address	Apt. #

City	State/Prov.	Zip/Postal Code

Signature (if under 18, a parent or guardian must sign)

Mail to the Harlequin® Reader Service:
IN U.S.A.: P.O. Box 1867, Buffalo, NY 14240-1867
IN CANADA: P.O. Box 609, Fort Erie, Ontario L2A 5X3

**Are you a subscriber to Love Inspired books
and want to receive the larger-print edition?
Call 1-800-873-8635 or visit www.ReaderService.com.**

* Terms and prices subject to change without notice. Prices do not include applicable taxes. Sales tax applicable in N.Y. Canadian residents will be charged applicable taxes. Offer not valid in Quebec. This offer is limited to one order per household. Not valid for current subscribers to Love Inspired books. All orders subject to credit approval. Credit or debit balances in a customer's account(s) may be offset by any other outstanding balance owed by or to the customer. Please allow 4 to 6 weeks for delivery. Offer available while quantities last.

Your Privacy—The Harlequin® Reader Service is committed to protecting your privacy. Our Privacy Policy is available online at www.ReaderService.com or upon request from the Harlequin Reader Service.
We make a portion of our mailing list available to reputable third parties that offer products we believe may interest you. If you prefer that we not exchange your name with third parties, or if you wish to clarify or modify your communication preferences, please visit us at www.ReaderService.com/consumerschoice or write to us at Harlequin Reader Service Preference Service, P.O. Box 9062, Buffalo, NY 14269. Include your complete name and address.

LIDIR13

ReaderService.com

Manage your account online!

- Review your order history
- Manage your payments
- Update your address

*We've designed
the Harlequin® Reader Service
website just for you.*

Enjoy all the features!

- Reader excerpts from any series
- Respond to mailings and special monthly offers
- Discover new series available to you
- Browse the Bonus Bucks catalog
- Share your feedback

Visit us at:

ReaderService.com